GOOD BLONDE & OTHERS

GOOD BLONDE & OTHERS
JACK KEROUAC

EDITED BY DONALD ALLEN
PREFACE BY ROBERT CREELEY

CITY LIGHTS/GREY FOX
SAN FRANCISCO

GOOD BLONDE & OTHERS © 1993, 1994 by John Sampas
Literary Representative

Thinking of Jack: A Preface © 1993 by Robert Creeley

Composition by Harvest Graphics

Cover photograph of Jack Kerouac © Allen Ginsberg/CORBIS
Cover design by Yolanda Montijo

Library of Congress Cataloging-in-Publication Data

Kerouac, Jack, 1922–1969.
    Good blonde & others / Jack Kerouac ; edited
By Donald Allen ; prefaced by Robert Creeley.

    p.   cm.
    ISBN: 0-912516-22-4
    ISBN 13: 978-0-912516-22-6
    1. Beat generation. I. Allen, Donald M.
II. Title. III. Title: Good blonde, and others.
PS3521.E735G6   1993   93-8063
814'.54 — dc20   CIP

GREY FOX is an imprint of CITY LIGHTS BOOKS.

Visit our website: www.citylights.com

CITY LIGHTS BOOKS are edited by Lawrence Ferlinghetti
and Nancy J. Peters and published at the City Lights
Bookstore, 261 Columbus Avenue, San Francisco, CA 94133.

Contents

Thinking of Jack: A Preface

The other night I had a dream that I was sitting on the sidewalk on Moody Street, Pawtucketville, Lowell, Mass., with a pencil and paper in my hand saying to myself "Describe the wrinkly tar of this sidewalk, also the iron pickets of Textile Institute, or the doorway where Lousy and you and G.J.'s always sittin and dont stop to think of words when you do stop, just stop to think of the picture better—and let your mind off yourself in this work."
—Dr. Sax

Jack Kerouac's Lowell was about fifteen miles from my own initial America, the small farm town West Acton, Massachusetts. Lowell, to the northeast, was the city where my family sometimes went for annual Easter clothes at the Bon Marche. On my mother's holidays we would go by the edge of it on our way up to see my Aunt Bernice who lived in what was then The Weirs in New Hampshire. The Boston and Maine Railroad was still another link, going through our town on its way to Chelmsford, and then Lowell just beyond, then on up to Nashua, Manchester, and finally to Canada, following along the river. It's all eastern, inland Massachusetts, old derelict mill towns, farms long ago abandoned to the suburbs, which nonetheless still echo in New England's habits to this day.

When I first met Jack in the spring of 1956, in San Francisco, we had each come a long way from that first world, yet still kept its company. I remember his friend Bob Donlin, also from there, saying, "There must be more people from Boston here than there are in Boston!" So it did seem. "On the road" was no simple tag or reflection of random travels but a state of necessary mind. We kept moving because there was, finally, no place we could come to rest. Always a build-

ing pressure of differences, of inability to find securing rela-
tions, to locate whatever would tie one usefully down, kept
the otherwise common world just that painful distance
beyond one's own reach or means to enter it. Reading now
these various pieces, with all their substantial details so char-
acteristic of Jack's work, I think of how particular and how
much a part of his way of being with others his attention really was—as if "to tell what subsequently I saw and what
heard," in W. C. Williams' phrase, were his own determined
gift to the people he lived with or just saw in passing. Again
it's that kind of *witness*, the kid who can tell what wonders
happened, the necessary audience for the heroic feats of the
mythic friend, who thus transforms the actual into the sub-
stance of its human fact. Jack was so exquisitely that person.
So when he travels with Robert Frank, who records with
camera all the "little details writers usually forget about,"
Jack himself notes each with his own pervasive gift of words:
"In darkening day, rain coming on the road, lights already on
at 3 PM, mist descending on Highway 40, we see the insect
swoop of modern sulphur lamps, the distant haze of forgotten
trees, the piled cars being tolled into the Baltimore Harbor
Tunnel, all of which Robert snaps casually while driving, one
eye to the camera, snap."

I've had other friends tell me that for them the camera was
a way of being with others, of having something to do that
got them past usual shyness and so into the company. The
stories, which began for Jack early, and the insistent commitment to recording what was there in front of him may well
have been his own means of keeping the world coherent and
at just enough distance to deal with. Liquor, of course, was
just another way of keeping it all at bay. Jack was certainly
shy, which I was much aware of, being shy too. We would
locate ourselves at the edge of the dancers, banging on
kitchen pots, drinking. My memory is that it felt like inten-

sive, defining participation, which is to say, I thought we were classically with it. But on one night, sitting at a table with Jack just in front of the small stand where Tommy Flannigan was playing with trio, I particularly so banged on the table with a beer bottle that I got us thrown out by the bouncer, Trent, whose identifying claim was he had been bodyguard for Dylan Thomas and also reputedly an FBI agent (?). Help! Jack was trying to ease me past him and out of the place, when Trent gave me one solid punch that drove an eyetooth solidly through my lip. Blood poured out but Jack got me clear, then to the small *pension* of some friends of his, French Canadians, who gave us use of a room to clean me up in, ice, towels, and a shot of brandy. Then Jack got me located with my friend Ann Hirshon, who had an apartment over in some housing project in another part of the city, after which he walked back over the Golden Gate Bridge to Locke McCorkle's house in Marin. Some days later, after I had spent the weekend in the Bryant Street jail, he figured it was time to get me out of the city for a break. One vivid moment I remember is Neal driving, Jack sitting in backseat, car wheeling through streets above North Beach, and Neal takes eyes off road to look at me, saying, "I'm worried about you, Bob." One forgets in the welter of usual report how particular such friendships really were.

So I went out to stay with Jack for a few days. Locke, his wife and family, were away seeing relatives and had left Jack to sit the house. Years later, after some blurred action in Palo Alto, I drove to that house with Ted Berrigan and Alice Notley, poets and friends then in Bolinas, just to show them where the parties had been, where Jack had often stayed, where Gary Snyder, Phil Whalen, Allen and Peter, all that old company had gathered. It was here that the great party to celebrate Gary's leaving first for Japan had taken place, ending with plunges into the surf off Stinson Beach, and Lew

Welch collecting mussels for instant lunch. It was in the cabin, with its open windows, Jack had sat listening to Ed Dorn's children talk, while watching a humming bird hover immaculately in just that place both in *and* outside the window's frame as though listening too. Jack had his small spiral notebook out, sat jotting, sketching it all with words.

Now, in the dark, we stood in the street looking up at the house—the small cabin sat too far up the hill back of it to be seen—with that pleasant musk of eucalyptus in the wet air. Momently a door on the deck built out from the house opened and someone appeared to say something I apparently heard wrongly. I thanked him nonetheless, said we had still some miles to go, and so couldn't come in, which I had taken him to have invited us to do. Somehow that time I'd known there, as if only our own lives finally mattered or counted, was long gone. Jack was dead and so was Neal. All of us had not so much changed as grown older.

Alice and Ted were laughing as we got back in the car, and it turned out the present person of the house hadn't been inviting us in at all. What he'd said was, "If you don't get out of here, I'll call the police!" So Ted and Alice later reported. Curious how I could change that to an hospitable invitation, but it was certainly a familiar greeting.

Ed Dorn speaks of Jack's having so worked the pronoun "I" so variously that its use now provokes of necessity some real question. What more can be done? He brought it as close in as one would seemingly be able to do, still keeping an outside possible. My first information of him was as the writer who had written a thousand pages of prose in which the only external, objectifying activity is a neon light going off and on above a store front. I'm sure he was more particular and you can find the reference, like they say. I think of his voice now, light on the ear, a bit soft, bemusing, in no way self-assertive. Gentle, I guess, without any intent to be so.

After the brief jail incident Jack gave me advice as to what I should do if arrested again. I was to tell the police I was a writer and they could then verify it by checking with the public library. I think he really believed they would. His own substantiating publication at that time was his first novel, *The Town and the City*. He felt writers were blessed people and I felt the same. I still do almost forty years later. If you know the powers of *Dr. Sax*, the way the mystifying world in which one is both young and helpless can be changed into securing enclosure—like the ring of a campfire or a family—then you will see how Jack Kerouac's powers so called the world into its obvious company, brought it literally to us who had otherwise felt only excluded. He spoke of his hope to write a series of novels which would tell the expanding story of his family, like Zola, but his "family" were the people of his life. Was that why Mamere, the mother who so enclosed him, was so valuable to him? Did she keep the hordes of us wanting his immaculate attention from exhausting himself altogether? I love the story Allen Ginsberg tells of trying to see him years later in Florida. He, Peter and Gregory have come to the house but when they knock they are met by his mother, who won't let them in. "Go away," she says, "you are bad boys. My Jack is a good boy. Leave him alone."

Then, of course, his peers in writing too often felt his work had no defining philosophy, no extricable "meaning," etc. Yet even then there was such a clear difference between a novel like Saul Bellow's *The Adventures of Augie Marsh* with its potted plot and persons as "examples," or else the later "adult" "children's book," *Catcher in the Rye*. Jack's was another story entirely. What it both wanted to do and did was to "take in" all that the senses apprehended, to move with the complexity of the moment's demand, to be "with it," as jazz was, not "about it" as authoritarian writing and criticism then argued. "Essentials of Spontaneous Prose" first appeared in the *Black*

Mountain Review's seventh and final issue (Autumn 1957). I
was the editor and Allen Ginsberg had just become an associ-
ate editor, joining Charles Olson and others. So the so-called
Black Mountain writers joined with the Beats, and Jack's con-
summate instance of what his note proposes, "October in the
Railroad Earth," appeared also together with Philip Whalen,
Michael McClure, William Burroughs, Gary Snyder and
Hubert Selby, Jr. Put simply, we all believed that whatever
way or form of writing we might use, its most articulate
means would be found as we then wrote, as we found then
and there the way to say it. No precedent "form" or precon-
ception could ever be there in the same way. Jazz was the
parallel. Our evident lives were the proof.

It cost a lot no doubt. Those "bad boys" (including Jack)
of Mamere's imagination were all of us in one real way or
another. We thought to be honest, like they say, to be true to
our own origins and persons, to break through the literary
habits and social determinants we felt our generation particularly to face. We took such risks as we could find as a badge
of honor. Security of any sort was a dirty word.

This book collects, then, what was always the point, hanging out, looking around, musing on life, caring for one's
friends, and finally making a living for oneself and those one
loves. It's a world with uninvested cares, common familiari-
ties, downhome pleasures. How far from the style of the period with all its careful culture, its self-conscious art, his now
seems. Where was the careful "literature" when that world
really did end, with an Eliotic "whimper" no less, despite
there was business as usual? Jack took it all, the exploitation
of his fame, his writing, his life. He tried to stay on the job
long after anyone seemed to be listening. He couldn't stand
it forever. In his biography of Jack Kerouac, Tom Clark
makes the point that magazines such as *Escapade* were those
few which had no prejudice against him. What he writes for

them has a preoccupation with "real life"—"real things and real people." ". . . I want to speak *for* things," he says in answer to Ben Hecht's sneering question in "Beatific." He sure did—once and for all, and forever.

Robert Creeley

Corolla, N.C.
April 8, 1993

On the Road

Good Blonde

This old Greek reminded me of my Uncle Nick in Brooklyn who'd spent 50 years of his life there after being born in Crete, and wandered down the gray streets of Wolfe Brooklyn, short, in a gray suit, with a gray hat, gray face, going to his various jobs as elevator operator and apartment janitor summer winter and fall, and was a plain old ordinary man talking about politics but with a Greek accent, and when he died it seemed to me Brooklyn hadn't changed and would never change, there would always be a strange sad Greek going down the gray streets. I could picture this man on the beach wandering around the white streets of San Francisco, looking at girls, "wandering around and looking at things as they are" as the Chinese say, "patting his belly," even, as Chuang-tse says. "I like these shells." He showed me a few shells he'd picked. "Make nice ashtray, I have lots ashtrays in my house."

"What do you think? You think all this is a dream?"

"What?"

"Life."

"Here? Now? What you mean a dream, we're awake, we talk, we see, we got eyes for to see the sea and the sand and the sky, if you dream you no see it."

"How we know we're not dreaming?"

"Look my eyes are open ain't they?" He watched me as I washed my dishes and put things away.

"I'm going to try to hitchhike to San Francisco or catch a freight, I don't wanta wait till tonight."

"You mens always in a hurry, hey, he he he he" and he laughed just like Old Uncle Nick, hands clasped behind his back, stooped slightly, standing over sand caves his feet had made, kicking little tufts of sand grass. In his green gray eyes which were just like the green gray sea I saw the yawning eternity not only of Greece but of America and myself.

"Well, I go now," says I hoisting my pack to my shoulder.

"I walk to the beach." Long before we'd stopped talking I'd seen the girl come out of the bushes, shameful and slow, and stroll on back to the bathhouse, then the boy came out, five minutes later. It made me sad I didn't have a girl to meet me in the bushes, in the exciting sand among leaves, to lie there swapping breathless kisses, groping at clothes, squeezing shoulders. Me and the old Greek sighed to see them sneak off. "I was a young man once," he said. At the bathhouse we shook hands and I went off across the mainline track to the little store on the corner were I'd bought the wine and where now they were playing a football game from Michigan loud on the radio and just then the sun came out anyway and I saw all the golden wheatfields of America Football Time stretching back to the East Coast.

"Damn," said I, "I'll just hitchhike on that highway" (101) seeing the fast flash of many cars. The old Greek was still wandering on the water's edge when I looked back, right on that mystical margin mentioned by Whitman where sea kisses sand in the endless sigh kiss of time. Like the three bos in Lordsburg New Mexico his direction in the void seemed so much sadder than my own, they were going east to hopeless sleeps in burlap in Alabama fields and the eventual Texas chaingang, he was going up and down the beach alone kicking sand . . . but I knew that in reality my own direction, going up to San Francisco to see the gang and whatever awaited me there, was no higher and no lower than his own humble and unsayable state. The little store had a tree in front, shade, I laid my pack down and went in and came out with a ten-cent ice cream on a stick and sat awhile eating, resting, then combed my hair with water out of an outside faucet and went to the highway all ready to thumb. I walked a few blocks up to the light and got on the far side and stood there, pack at my feet, for a good half hour during which time I got madder and madder and finally I was swearing to myself "I will never hitchhike again, it's getting worse and worse every goddamn year." Meanwhile I kept a sharp eye on the rails a block toward the sea watching for convenient freight trains. At the moment when I was the maddest, and was standing there, thumb out, completely infuriated and so much so that (I remember) my eyes were slitted, my teeth clenched, a brand new cinnamon colored Lincoln driven by a beautiful young blonde in a bathingsuit flashed by and suddenly swerved to the right and put to a stop in the side of the road for me. I couldn't believe it. I figured she wanted road information. I picked up my pack and ran. I opened the door and looked in to smile and thank her.

She said "Get in. Can you drive?" She was a gorgeous young blonde girl of about 22 in a pure white bathingsuit, barefooted with a little ankle bracelet around her right ankle. Her bathingsuit was shoulderless and low cut. She sat there in the luxurious cinnamon sea in that white suit like a model. In fact she was a model. Green eyes, from Texas, on her way back to the City.

"Sure I can drive but I don't have a license."

"You drive all right?"

"I drive as good as anybody."

"Well I'm dog tired, I've been driving all the way from Texas without sleep, I went to see my family there" (by now she had the heap jet gone up the road and went up to 60 and kept it there hard and clean on the line, driving like a good man driver). "Boy," she said, "I sure wish I had some Benzedrine or sumptin to keep me awake. I'll have to give you the wheel pretty soon."

"Well how far you going?"

"Far as you are I think . . . San Francisco."

"Wow, great." (To myself: who will ever believe I got a ride like this from a beautiful chick like that practically naked in a bathingsuit, wow, what does she expect me to do next?) "And Benzedrine you say?" I said "I've got some here in my bag, I just got back from Mexico, I got plenty."

"Crazy!" she yelled. "Pull it out. I want some."

"Baby you'll drive all the way when you get high on that stuff, Mexican you know."

"Mexican Shmexican just give it to me."

"OK." Grinning I began dumping all my dirty old un-washed rags and gear and claptraps of cookpot junk and pieces of food in wrapper on the floor of her car searching feverishly for the little tubes of Benny suddenly I couldn't find anymore. I began to panic. I looked in all the flaps and sidepockets. "Goddamnit where is it!" I kept worrying the smell of my old unwashed clothes would be repugnant to her, I wanted to find the stuff as soon as possible and repack everything away.

"Never mind man, take your time," she said looking straight ahead at the road, and in a pause in my search I let my eye wander to her ankle bracelet, as damaging a sight as Cleopatra on her poop of beaten gold, and the sweet little snowy bare foot on the gas pedal, enough to drive a man mad. I kept wondering why she'd really picked me up.

I asked her "How come you picked up a guy like me? I never seen a girl alone pick up a guy."

"Well I tell you I need someone to help me drive to the City and I figured you could drive, you looked like it anyway . . ."

"O where are those Bennies!"

"Take your time."

"Here they are!"

"Crazy! I'll pull into that station up ahead and we'll go in and have a Coke and swallow em down." She pulled into the station which also had an inside luncheonette. She jumped out of the car barefooted in her low-cut bathingsuit as the attendant stared and ordered a full tank as I went in and bought two bottles of Coke to go out, cold. When I came back she was in the car with her change, ready to go. What a wild chick. I looked at the attendant to see what he was thinking. He was looking at me enviously. I kept having the urge to tell him the true story.

"Here," and I handed her the tubes, and she took out two. "Hey, that's too many, your top'll fly out . . . better take one and a half, or one. I take one myself."

"I don't want no one and a half, I want two."

"You've had it before?"

"Of course man and everything else."

"Pot too?"

"Sure pot . . . I know all the musicians in L.A. and the City, when I come into the Ramador Shelly Manne sees me coming and stops whatever they're playing and they play my theme song which is a little bop arrangement."

"How does it go?"

"Ha! and it goes: boop boop be doodleya dap."

"Wow, you can sing."

"I walk in, man, and they play that, and everybody knows I'm back." She took her two Bennies and swigged down, and buzzed the car up to a steady 70 as we hit the country north of Santa Barbara, the traffic thinning and the road getting longer and straighter. "Long drive to San Francisco, four hundred miles just about. I hope these Bennies are good, I'd like to go all the way."

"Well if you're tired I can drive," I said but hoped I wouldn't have to drive, the car was so brand new and beautiful. It was a '55 Lincoln and here it was October 1955. Beautiful, lowslung, sleek. Zip, rich. I leaned back with my

Benny in my palm and threw it down with the Coke and felt good. Up ahead suddenly I realized the whole city of San Francisco would be all bright lights and glittering wide open waiting for me this very night, and no strain, no hurt, no pain, no freight train, no sweating on the hitchhike road but up there zip zoom inside about eight hours. She passed cars smoothly and went on. She turned on the radio and began looking for jazz, found rock 'n' roll and left that on, loud. The way she looked straight ahead and drove with no expression and sending no mincing gestures my way or even telepathies of mincingness, you'd never believe she was a lovely little chick in a bathingsuit. I was amazed. And in the bottom of that scheming mind I kept wondering and wondering (dirtily) if she hadn't picked me up because she was secretly a sex-fiend and was waiting for me to say "Let's park the car somewhere and make it" but something so inviolately grave about her prevented me from saying this, more than that my own sudden bashfulness (as the holy Benny began taking effect) prevented me from making such an importunate and really insulting proposition seeing I'd just met the young lady. But the thought stuck and stuck with me. I was afraid to turn and look at her and only occasionally dropped my eyes to that ankle bracelet and the little white lily foot on the gas pedal. And we talked and talked. Finally the Benny began hitting us strong after Los Alamos and we were talking a blue streak, she did most of the talking. She'd been a model, she wanted to be an actress, so forth, the usual beautiful-California-blonde designs but finally I said "As for me I don't want any-thing . . . I think life is suffering, a suffering dream, and all I wanta do is rest and be kind somewhere, preferably in the woods, under a tree, live in a shack."

"Ain't you ever gonna get married?"

"Been married twice and I've had it."

"Well you oughta take a third crack at it, maybe this time

you'd hit a homerun."

"That ain't the point, in the first place I wouldn't wanta have children, they only born to die."

"You better not tell that to my mom and dad, they had eight kids in Texas, I was the second, they've had a damn good long life and the kids are great, you know what my youngest brother did when I walked in the house last week and hadn't seen him for a year: he was all grown up tall and put on a rock-'n'-roll record for me and wanted me to do the lindy with him. O what laughs we had in the old homestead last week. I'm glad I went."

"I'll bet when you were a little girl you had a ball there in Texas huh? hunting, wandering around."

"Everything man, sometimes I think my new life now modeling and acting in cities isn't half as good as that was."

"And there you were on long Texas nights Grandma readin the Bible, right?"

"Yeah and all the good food we made, nowadays I have dates in good restaurants and man — "

"Dates . . . you ain't married hey?"

"Not yet, pretty soon."

"Well what does a beautiful girl like you think about?" This made her turn and look at me with bland frank green eyes.

"What do you mean?"

"I don't know . . . I'd say, for a man, like me, what I say is best for him . . . but for a beautiful girl like you I guess what you're doing is best." I wasn't going to say get thee to a nunnery, she was too gone, too pretty too, besides she wouldn't have done it by a long shot, she just didn't care. In no time at all we were way up north of Los Alamos and coming into a little bumper to bumper traffic outside Santa Maria where she pulled up at a gas station and said:

"Say do you happen to have a little change?"

"About a dollar and a half."

"Hmmmm . . . I want to call longdistance to South City and tell my man I'll be in at eight or so."

"Call him collect if he's your man."

"Now you're talkin like a man" she said and went trottin barefoot to the phone booth in the driveway and got in and made a call with a dime. I got out of the car to stretch out, high and dizzy and pale and sweating and excited from the Benzedrine, I could see she was the same way in the phone booth, chewing vigorously on a wad of gum. She got her call and talked while I picked up an orange from the ground and wound up and did the pitcher-on-the-mound bit to stretch my muscles. I felt good. A cool wind was blowing across Santa Maria, with a smell of the sea in it somehow. The palm trees waved in a cooler wind than the one in Barbara and L.A. Tonight it would be the cool fogs of Frisco again! After all these years! She came out and we got in.

"Who's the guy."

"He's my man, Joey King, he runs a bar in South City . . . on Main Street."

"Say I used to be a yardclerk in the yards there and I'd go to some of those bars on Main Street for a beer . . . with a little cocktail glass neon in front, with a stick in it?"

"All the bars have that around here," she laughed and gunned on up the road fast. Pretty soon, yakking happily about jazz and even singing a lot of jazz, we got to San Luis Obispo, went through town, and started up the pass to Santa Margarita.

"There you see it," I said, "see where the railroad track winds around to go up the pass, I was a brakeman on that for years, on drizzly nights I'd be squattin under lumber boards ridin up that pass and when I'd go through the tunnels I'd hold my bandanna over my nose not to suffocate."

"Why were you riding on the outside of the engine."

"Because I was the guy assigned to puttin pops up and down, air valves, for mountain brakes, all that crap . . . I don't think it would interest you."

"Sure, my brother's a brakeman in Texas. He's about your age."

"I'm thirty-three."

"Well he's a little younger but his eyes are greener than yours, yours are blue."

"Yours are green."

"No, mine are hazel."

"Well that's what green-eyed girls always say."

"What do hazel-eyed girls always say?"

"They say, hey now." We were (as you see) talking like two kids and completely unself-conscious and by this time I'd quite forgotten the lurking thought of us sexing together in some bushes by the side of the road, though I kept smelling her, the Benny sweat, which is abundant, and perfumy in the way it works, it filled the car with a sweet perfume, mingled with my own sweat, in our noses if not in our minds there was a thought of sweating love . . . at least in my mind. Sometimes I felt the urge to just lay my head in her lap as she drove but then I got mad and thought "Ah hell it's all a dream including beauty, leave the Angel Alone you dirty old foney Duluoz" which I did. To this day I never know what she wanted, I mean, what she really secretly thought of me, of picking me up, and she got so high on the Benny she drove all the way anyway, or perhaps she woulda drove all the way anyway, I don't know. She balled up over the pass in the gathering late afternoon golden shadows of California and came out on the flats of the Margarita plateau, where we stopped for gas, where in the rather cool mountain wind she got out and ran to the ladies room and the gas attendant said to me:

"Where'd you pick her up?" thinking the car was mine.

"She picked *me* up, pops."

"Well I oughta be glad if I was you."

"I ain't unglad."

"Sure is a nice little bundle."

"She's been wearing that bathingsuit clear from Texas."

"Geez." She came out and we went up the Salinas valley as it got dark slowly with old orange sunsets behind the rim where I'd seen bears as a brakeman, at night, standing by the track as we'd in the Diesel ball by with a hundred-car freight behind us, and one time a cougar. Wild country. And the floor of the dry Salinas riverbottom is all clean white sand and bushes, ideal for bhikkuing (outdoor camping where nobody bothers you) because you can hide good and hide your campfire and the only people to bother you are cattle, and snakes I guess, and beautiful dry climate with stars, even now at dusk, I could see flashing in the pale plank of heaven, like bhaghavat nails. I told Pretty about it:

"Someday I'm gonna bring my pack and a month's essential groceries right down to that riverbottom and build a little shelter with twigs and stuff and a tarpaulin or a poncho and lay up and do nothing for a month."

"What you wanta do that for? There's no fun in that."

"Sure there is."

"Well I can't figure all this out but . . . it's all right I guess." At times I didn't like her, at one point I definitely didn't like her because there was something so cold and yawny distant about her, I felt that in her secret bedroom she probably yawned a lot and didn't know what to do with herself and to compensate for that had a lot of boyfriends who bought her expensive presents (just because she was beautiful, which compensated not for her inside unbeautiful feeling), and going to restaurants and bars and jazz clubs and yooking it up because there was nothing else inside. And I thought: "Truly, I'm better off *without* a doll like this . . . out there in that riverbottom, pure and free, what immensities I'd have, in real riches . . . alone, in old clothes, cooking my own food, finding my own peace . . . instead of sniffin around her ankles day in day out wonderin whether in some mean mood she's going to throw me out anyway and then I would have to clap her one or something and all of it a crock for sure — " I didn't dare tell her all this, besides the point being she wouldn't have been interested in the least. It got dark, we flew on, soon we saw the sealike flats of Salinas valley stretching on both sides of us, with occasional brown farmlamps, the stars overhead, a vast storm cloud gathering in the night sky in the east and the radio announcer predicting rain for the night, then finally far up ahead the jeweled cluster of Salinas the city and airport lights. Outside Salinas on the four lane, about five miles, suddenly she said "The car's run out of gas, Oho" and she began wobbling the car from side to side in a graceful dance.

"What you doin that for?"

"That's to splash what's left of the gas into the carburetor . . . I can do this for a few miles, let's pray we see a station or we don't get to South City by eight." She swayed and wobbled along, grinning faintly over her wheel, and in the cuddly dark and little emergency of the night, I began to love her again and thought "Ah well and what a strong sweet angel to spend the rest of your life with, though, damn." Pretty soon the wobbles were wider and the speed slower and she finally pulled over by the side of the road and parked and said "That's that, we're out of gas."

"I'll go out and hail a car."

"While you're doing that I'll go in the backseat and put something over my bathingsuit, it's getting cold," which it was. I unsuccessfully tried to hail down cars for five minutes or so, they were all zipping at a steady 70, and I said:

"Say when you're ready come on out, when they see *you* they'll stop." She came out and we joked a bit in the dark dancing and showing our legs at the cars and finally a big truck stopped and I ran after it to talk to him. It was a big burly guy eager to help, he'd seen the blond. He got out a chain and tied her car on and off we went at about 15 miles per hour to the gas station three miles down. He had air-brakes and she was worried about ramming him and hoped he wouldn't go too fast. He went perfect. In the gas station driveway he got out to admire her some more.

"Boy, that's a little bit of sumptin" he said to me as she went to the toilet.

"She picked me up in Santa Barbara, she's been driving all the way from Texas alone."

"Well, well, you're a luck hitchhiker." He undid the chain. She came out and stood around chatting with the big truck-driver and the attendant. Now she was clad in tightfitting black slacks and a neat keen throwover of some kind, and sandals, in which she padded like a little tightfit Indian. I felt humble and foolish with the two men staring at her and me waiting by the car for my poor world ride. She came back and off we went, getting through Salinas and out on the dark road and now finally we found some real fine jazz from San Francisco, the Pat Henry show or some other show, and we didn't speak much anymore but just sang with the music and kept our eyes glued on the headlamp swatch and the inwinding kiss-in of the white line in the road where it again became a two-laner. Soon we were going through Watsonville, a little behind schedule.

"Here's where I did most of my work as a brakeman . . . insteada sleeping in the railroad dormitory I'd go out to the sandbottom of that river, the Pajaro, and cook woodfires and eat hotdogs like last night and sleep in the sand . . ."

"You're always in some riverbottom or other." The music on the radio got louder and louder as we began to approach San Jose and the City. The storm to the east hadn't formed yet. It was exciting to be coming into the City now. On Bayshore we really felt it, all the cars flashing by both ways in the lanes, the lights, the roadside restaurants, the antennas, nothing had looked like that all day, the big city, "The Apple," I said, "the Apple of California but have you ever been to *the* Apple, New York!" to which she replied: "Yeah man."

"But nothing wrong with this little old town, it's got everything . . . isn't it . . . don't you feel a funny feeling in your belly coming into the City."

"Yeah man I always do." We agreed on that and talked about it, and soon we were coming into South San Francisco where I suddenly realized she was going to let me out in a few minutes and I hadn't anticipated parting from her ever, somehow. She pulled up right smack in front of the little station where I'd worked as a yardclerk and there were the same old tracks, I knew every number and name of them, and the same old overpass, and the spurs leading off to the slaughterhouses Armour and Swift east, the same sad lamps and sad dim red switchlights in the darkness. The car stopped, our bodies were still vibrating as we sat in the stillness, the radio booming.

"Well I'll get out and let you get home," I said, "and I needn't tell you how great it was and how glad I am you gave me this great ride."

"Oh man, nothing, it was fun."

"Why don't you give me your phone, I'll call you and we'll go down and hear Brue Moore, I hear he's in town."

"O he's my favorite tenor, I've seen him . . . OK, I'll give you my address, I haven't got a phone in yet."

"OK." She wrote out the address in my little breastpocket notebook and I could see she was anxious to get on home to her man so I said "OK, here I go," and got my bag and went out and stuck my hand in to shake and off she went, up Main Street, probably to her pad to take a shower and dress up and go down to her man's bar. And I put my bag on my

back and walked down the same old homey familiar rail and
felt glad . . . probably gladder than she did, but who knows?
It almost brought tears to my eyes to see my old railyards
again, as though I'd been brought up to them on a magic car-
pet just to see them and remember, the whole trip had been
so ephemeral and easy and fast, in fact the whole trip from
Mexico City 4000 gory miles away . . . as though some ruling
God in the sky had said "Jack I want you to cry when you
remember your past life, and to accomplish this, I'm going to
shoot you to that spot" and there I was, walking numbly on
the same old railside cinders and there across the way the
long sorrowful pink neon saying BETHLEHEM WEST
COAST STEEL about five long blocks of it and I used to
take down the numbers of boxcars and gons in drags that
were even longer than that and measure their length by the
length of the huge neon: beyond which you could hear frogs
croaking in the airport marsh, where mountains of tin scrap
soaked in scum water, and rats scurried, and occasional pure
Chinese birds sailed around (at night, bats). I went into the
old station (actually a brand new little station still fresh with
new bricks) and consulted the timetable and saw that I had a
train to the City in five minutes, everything perfect. As of
yore, to celebrate, I stuck a nickel in my old candy machine
and got out a Pay Day and munched on that on the platform,
stole a newspaper from the rack, and it was just like old times
11:15 going home with work done. But the train had
changed, it came being pulled by a new type of small engine
I'd never seen (electric) and the cars were doubledeckers
with commuters sitting up and below like dolls in the bright
lights of the new ceilings. "Too new, too fancy" I thought,
regretting it, and got on and got my ticket punched by a con-
ductor whose face I vaguely remembered from the trainmen's
lockers at Third and Townsend. On we went to the City.
Bayshore Yards appeared after a while, with the old redbrick

1890 roundhouse gloomy like *Out Our Way* cartoons of 1930 factories in the night, smoke of steampots beyond, the distant marvel and visible miracle of Oakland suddenly seen casting its infinitesimal and as-if-innumerable lights on the far bay waters, and then swosh into the tunnel, coming out right smack in the City with white tenements and houses on grassy cliffs by the side of the dug-in rail canyon, and then the long slow curve, the long slow appearance of the skyscrapers of downtown San Francisco, so sad, so reddish, so mysterious and Chinese, and the general purple brownness of the yards, red and green switchlights, funny switchmen at the crossings and the train slowing down as it comes into the station to the deadend blocks to stop.

Everybody got up and got out. I went slowly to savor everything. The smell of San Francisco was great, it is always the same, at night, a compoundment of sea, fog, cinders, coalsmoke, taffy and dust. And somehow the smell of wine, maybe from all the broken bottles on Third Street. Now I was really exhausted and headed up Third Street, after a slow nostalgic survey of the Third and Townsend station, looking desultorily if there was anybody I knew, like maybe Cody, or Mal. I went straight to the little old Cameo Hotel on the corner of Harrison and Third, where for 75 cents a night you could always get a clean room with no bedbugs and nice soft mattresses with soft old clean sheets, clean enough, not snow-white Fab by any means but better, and nice quilts, and old frayed carpets and quiet sleep: that's the main thing. The clerk in the cage was the same Hindu I'd known there in 1954, he didn't remember me or the night he'd told me the long story of his boyhood in India and his father who owned 700 camels and the time he'd peeked at a woman's religious ritual where he claimed there were some virgins and barren women walking around a stone phallus and sitting on it. I didn't bring it up but followed him up the stairs and down the sad old hall to my door, and the room. I took all my clothes off and got in the cool smooth sheets and said "Now I'll just lay like this for fifteen minutes in the dark and rest and then I'll get up, dress and go down to Chinatown and have a nice feed: I'll have sweet and sour prawn and cold broiled duck, yessir, I'll splurge a dollar and a half on that" and I uncapped my little poorboy of tokay wine I'd bought in the store downstairs and took a swig and in fifteen minutes, after three swigs and dreamy thoughts with a serene smile realizing I was at last back in my beloved San Francisco and surely must have a lot of crazy adventures ahead of me, I was asleep. And slept the sleep of the justified.

Introduction to *The Americans:*
Photographs by Robert Frank

That crazy feeling in america when the sun is hot on the streets and music comes out of the jukebox or from a nearby funeral, that's what Robert Frank has captured in these tremendous photographs taken as he traveled on the road around practically forty-eight states in an old used car (on Guggenheim Fellowship) and with the agility, mystery, genius, sadness and strange secrecy of a shadow photographed scenes that have never been seen before on film. For this he will definitely be hailed as a great artist in his field. After seeing these pictures you end up finally not knowing any more whether a jukebox is sadder than a coffin. That's because he's always taking pictures of jukeboxes and coffins — and intermediary mysteries like the Negro priest squatting underneath the bright liquid belly *mer* of the Mississippi at Baton Rouge for some reason at dusk or early dawn with a white snowy cross and secret incantations never known outside the bayou — Or the picture of a chair in some cafe with the sun coming in the window and setting on the chair in a holy halo I never thought could be caught on film much less described in its beautiful visual entirety in words.

The humor, the sadness, the EVERYTHING-ness and American-ness of these pictures! Tall thin cowboy rolling butt outside Madison Square Garden New York for rodeo season, sad, spindly, unbelievable — Long shot of night road arrowing forlorn into immensities and flat of impossible-to-believe America in New Mexico under the prisoner's moon — under the whang whang guitar star — Haggard old frowsy dames of Los Angeles leaning peering out the right front window of Old Paw's car on a Sunday gawking and criticizing to explain Amerikay to little children in the spattered back seat — tattoed guy sleeping on grass in park in Cleveland, snoring dead to the world on a Sunday afternoon with too many balloons and sailboats — Hoboken in the winter, platform full of politicians all ordinary looking till suddenly at the far end to the right you see one of them pursing his lips in prayer politico (yawning probably) not a soul cares — Old man standing hesitant with oldman cane under old steps long since torn down — Madman resting under American flag canopy in old busted car seat in fantastic Venice California backyard, I could sit in it and sketch 30,000 words (as a railroad brakeman I rode by such backyards leaning out of the old steam pot) (empty tokay bottles in the palm weeds) — Robert picks up two hitchhikers and lets them drive the car, at night, and people look at their two faces looking grimly onward into the night ("Visionary Indian angels who *were* visionary Indian angels" says Allen Ginsberg) and people say "Ooo how mean they look" but all they want to do is arrow on down that road and get back to the sack — Robert's here to tell us so — St. Petersburg Florida the retired old codgers on a bench in the busy mainstreet leaning on their canes and talking about social security and one incredible I think Seminole half Negro woman pulling on her cigarette with thoughts of her own, as pure a picture as the nicest tenor solo in jazz . . .

As American a picture — the faces dont editorialize or criticize or say anything but "This is the way we are in real life and if you dont like it I dont know anything about it 'cause I'm living my own life my way and may God bless us all, mebbe" . . . "if we deserve it" . . .

Oi the lone woe of Lee Lucien, a basketa pittykats . . .

What a poem this is, what poems can be written about this book of pictures some day by some young new writer high by candlelight bending over them describing every gray myste-

rious detail, the gray film that caught the actual pink juice of
human kind. Whether 't is the milk of humankind-ness, of
human-kindness, Shakespeare meant, makes no difference
when you look at these pictures. Better than a show.
Madroad driving men ahead — the mad road, lonely, leading around the bend into the openings of space towards the
horizon Wasatch snows promised us in the vision of the west,
spine heights at the world's end, coast of blue Pacific starry
night — nobone half-banana moons sloping in the tangled
night sky, the orments of great formations in mist, the huddled invisible insect in the car racing onward, illuminate
— The raw cut, the drag, the butte, the star, the draw, the
sunflower in the grass — orangebutted west lands of Arcadia,
forlorn sands of the isolate earth, dewy exposures to infinity
in black space, home of the rattlesnake and the gopher — the
level of the world, low and flat: the charging restless mute
unvoiced road keening in a seizure of tarpaulin power into
the route, fabulous plots of landowners in green unexpecteds, ditches by the side of the road, as I look. From here to
Elko along the level of this pin parallel to telephone poles I
can see a bug playing in the hot sun — swush, hitch yourself
a ride beyond the fastest freight train, beat the smoke, find
the thighs, spend in the shiney, throw the shroud, kiss the
morning star in the morning glass — madroad driving men
ahead. Pencil traceries of our faintest wish in the travel of the
horizon merged, nosey cloud obfusks in a drabble of speechless distance, the black sheep clouds cling a parallel above
the steams of C.B.Q. — serried Little Missouri rocks haunt
the badlands, harsh dry brown fields roll in the moonlight
with a shiny cow's ass, telephone poles toothpick time, "dotting immensity" the crazed voyageur of the lone automobile
presses forth his eager insignificance in noseplates & licenses
into the vast promise of life. Drain your basins in old Ohio
and the Indian and the Illini plains, bring your Big Muddy

rivers thru Kansas and the mudlands, Yellowstone in the frozen North, punch lake holes in Florida and L.A., *raise* your cities in the white plain, cast your mountains up, bedawze the west, bedight the west with brave hedgerow cliffs rising to Promethean heights and fame — plant your prisons in the basin of the Utah moon — nudge Canadian groping lands that end in Arctic bays, purl your Mexican ribneck, America — we're going home, going home.

Lying on his satin pillow in the tremendous fame of death, Man, black, mad mourners filing by to take a peek at Holy Face to see what death is like and death is like life, what else? — If you know what the sutras say — Chicago convention with sleek face earnest wheedling confiding cigarholding union boss fat as Nero and eager as Caesar in the thunderous beer crash hall leaning over to confide — Gaming table at Butte Montana with background election posters and little gambling doodads to knock over, editorial page in itself —

Car shrouded in fancy expensive designed tarpolian (I knew a truckdriver pronounced it "tarpolian") to keep soots of no-soot Malibu from falling on new simonize job as owner who is a two-dollar-an-hour carpenter snoozes in house with wife and TV, all under palm trees for nothing, in the cemeterial California night, ag, ack — In Idaho three crosses where the cars crashed, where that long thin cowboy just barely made it to Madison Square Garden as he was about a mile down the road then — *"I told you to wait in the car"* say people in America so Robert sneaks around and photographs little kids waiting in the car, whether three little boys in a motorama limousine, ompious & opiful, or poor little kids can't keep their eyes open on Route 90 Texas at 4 A.M. as dad goes to the bushes and stretches — The gasoline monsters stand in the New Mexico flats under big sign says SAVE — the sweet little white baby in the black nurse's arms both of them bemused in Heaven, a picture that should have been blown up and hung in the street of Little Rock showing love under the sky and in the womb of our universe the Mother — And the loneliest picture ever made, the urinals that women never see, the shoeshine going on in sad eternity —

Wow, and blown over Chinese cemetery flowers in a San Francisco hill being hammered by potatopatch fog on a March night I'd say nobody there but the rubber cat —

Anybody doesnt like these pitchers dont like potry, see? Anybody dont like potry go home see Television shots of big hatted cowboys being tolerated by kind horses.

Robert Frank, Swiss, unobtrusive, nice, with that little camera that he raises and snaps with one hand he sucked a sad poem right out of America onto film, taking rank among the tragic poets of the world.

To Robert Frank I now give this message: You got eyes.

And I say: That little ole lonely elevator girl looking up sighing in an elevator full of blurred demons, what's her name & address?

On the Road to Florida

Just took a trip by car to Florida with Photographer Robert
Frank, Swiss born, to get my mother and cats and typewriter
and big suitcase full of original manuscripts, and we took this
trip on a kind of provisional assignment from *Life* magazine
who gave us a couple hundred bucks which paid for the gas
and oil and chow both ways. But I was amazed to see how a
photographic artist does the bit, of catching those things
about the American Road writers write about. It's pretty
amazing to see a guy, while steering at the wheel, suddenly
raise his little 300-dollar German camera with one hand and
snap something that's on the move in front of him, and
through an unwashed windshield at that. Later on, when
developed, the unwashed streaks dont harm the light, composition or detail of the picture at all, seem to enhance it. We
started off in N. Y. at noon of a pretty Spring day and didnt
take any pictures till we had negotiated the dull but useful
stretch of the New Jersey Turnpike and come on down to
Highway 40 in Delaware where we stopped for a snack in a
roadside diner. I didnt see anything in particular to photograph, or "write about," but suddenly Robert was taking his
first snap. From the counter where we sat, he had turned and
taken a picture of a big car-trailer with piled cars, two tiers,
pulling in the gravel driveyard, but through the window and
right over a scene of leftovers and dishes where a family had
just vacated a booth and got in their car and driven off, and
the waitress not had time yet to clear the dishes. The combination of that, plus the movement outside, and further
parked cars, and reflections everywhere in chrome, glass and
steel of cars, cars, road, road, I suddenly realized I was taking
a trip with a genuine artist and that he was expressing him-

self in an art-form that was not unlike my own and yet fraught with a thousand difficulties quite unlike those of my own. Contrary to the general belief about photography, you don't need bright sunlights: the best, moodiest pictures are taken in the dim light of almost-dusk, or of rainy days, like it was now in Delaware, late afternoon with rain impending in the sky and lights coming on on the road. Outside the diner, seeing nothing as usual, I walked on, but Robert suddenly stopped and took a picture of a solitary pole with a cluster of silver bulbs way up on top, and behind it a lorn American Landscape so unspeakably indescribable, to make a Marcel Proust shudder . . . how beautiful to be able to detail a scene like that, on a gray day, and show even the mud, abandoned tin cans and old building blocks laid at the foot of it, and in the distance the road, the old going road with its trucks, cars, poles, roadside houses, trees, signs, crossings. . . A truck pulls into the gravel flat, Robert plants himself in front of it and catches the driver in his windshield wild-eyed and grinning mad like an Indian. He catches that glint in his eye. . . He takes a picture of a fantastic truck door announcing all the licenses from Arkansas to Washington, Florida to Illinois, with its confusion of double mirrors arranged so the driver can see to the rear around the body of the trailer . . . little details writers usually forget about. In darkening day, rain coming on the road, lights already on at 3 PM, mist descending on Highway 40, we see the insect swoop of modern sulphur lamps, the distant haze of forgotten trees, the piled cars being tolled into the Baltimore Harbor Tunnel, all of which Robert snaps casually while driving, one eye to the camera, snap. Thence down into Maryland, lights flashing now in a 4 PM rain, the lonely look of a crossroad stoplight, the zing of telephone wires into the glooming distance where another truck heads obstinately toward some kind of human goal, of zest, or rest. And GULF, the big sign, in the gulf of time . . . a not unusual yet somehow always startling sight in all the pure hotdog roadstand and motel whiteness in a nameless district of U. S. A. where red traffic lights always seem to give a sense of rain and green traffic lights a sense of distance, snow, sand. . .

Then the colored girl laughing as she collects the dollar toll at the Potomac River Bridge at dusk, the toll being registered in lights on the board. Then over the bridge, the flash and mystery of oncoming car lights (something a writer using words can never quite get), the sense of old wooden jetties however unphotographable far below rotting in the mud and bushes, the old Popomac into Virginia, the scene of old Civil War battles, the crossing into the country known as The Wilderness, all a sadness of steel a mile long now as the waters roll on anyway, mindless of America's mad invention, photographs, words. The glister of rain on the bridge paving, the reds of brakelights, the gray reflections from open holes in the sky with the sun long gone behind rain to the westward hills of Maryland. You're in the South now.

A dreary thing to drive through Richmond Virginia in a drenching midnight downpour.

But in the morning, after a little sleep, America wakes up for you again in the bright morning sun, fresh grass and the hitchhiker flat on his back sleeping in the sun, with his carton suitcase and coat before him, as a car goes by on the road — he knows he'll get there anyway, if at all, why not sleep. His America. And beyond his sleep, the old trees and the long A. C. L. freight balling on by on the main line, and patches of sand in the grass. I sit in the car amazed to see the photographic artist prowling like a cat, or an angry bear, in the grass and roads, shooting whatever he wants to see. How I wished I'd have had a camera of my own, a mad mental camera that could register pictorial shots, of the photographic artist himself prowling about for his ultimate shot — an epic in itself.

We drove down into Rocky Mount North Carolina where, at a livestock auction right outside town, hundreds of out-of-work Southerners of the present recession milled about in the Russia-looking mud staring at things like the merchant's clutter of wares in the back trunk of his fintail new-car . . . there he sits, before his tools, drills, toothpaste, pipe tobacco, rings, screwdrivers, fountain pens, gloomy and jut jawed and sad, in the gray Southern day, as livestock moo and moan within and everywhere the cold sense of drizzle and hopelessness. "I should imagine," said Robert Frank to me that morning over coffee, "though I've never been to Russia, that America is really more like Russia, in feeling and look, than any other country in the world . . . the big distances, the faces, the look of families traveling. . . "We drove on, down near South Carolina got out of the car to catch a crazy picture of a torndown roadside eatery that still announced "Dinner is ready, this is It, welcome" and you could see through the building to the fields the other side and around it bulldozers wrecking and working.

In a little town in South Carolina, as we floated by in the car, as I steered for him slowly down Main Street, he leaned from the driver's window and caught three young girls coming home from school. In the sun. Their complaint: "O Jeez."

Further down, the little girl in the front seat with pin curls, her mother doubleparked in front of some Five and Ten.

A car parked near a diner near a junkyard further down, and in the back seat, strung to a necessary leash, a frightened little cat . . . the pathos of the road and of Modern America: "What am I doing in all this junk?"

We went off our route a little to visit Myrtle Beach, South Carolina, and got a girl being very pensive leaning on the pinball machine watching her boy's score.

A little down the road to McClellanville South Carolina, scene of beautiful old houses and incredible peace, and the old "Coastal Barber Shop" run by 80 year old Mr. Bryan who proudly declared "I was the first white barber in McClellanville." We asked him where in town we could get a cup of coffee. "Aint no place, but you go down to the sto and get you a jar of powder coffee and bring it back, I got a nice pot on the stove here and got three cups..." Mr. Bryan lived on the highway a few miles away, where, "All's I like to do is sit on my porch and watch the cars run." Wanted to make a trade for Robert Frank's 1952 Stationwagon. "Got a nice Thirty Six Ford and another car." "How old is the other car?" "It aint quite as young ... but you boys need two cars, dont ya? You goin to get married, aint ya?" Insists on giving us haircuts. With comb in the hair in the old barber tradition, he gives the photographer a weird haircut and chuckles and reminisces. Barber shop hasnt changed since Photographer Frank was by here about five years ago to photograph the shop from the street door, even the bottles on the shelf are all the same and apparently havent been moved.

A little ways down a country road, to the colored houses of McClellanville, a Negro funeral, Strawhat Charley with razor scar looking out the window of his black shiny car, "Yay"... And the graves, simple mounds covered with clam shells, sometimes one symbolic Coca Cola bottle. Things you cant capture in words, the moody poem of death...

A little more sleep, and Savannah in the morning. Prowling around we see a brand new garbage truck of the City of Savannah with fantastic propped-up dolls' heads that blink their eyes as the truck lumbers through back alleys and women in their bathrobes come out and supervise ... the dolls, the American flag, the horseshoe in the windshield, the emblems, mirrors, endless pennons and admirable spears, and the boss driver himself, colored, all decked out in boots and cap and a "garbage" knife in his belt. He says "Wait here till we come around the corner and you catch a pitcher of the truck in the SUN" and Robert Frank obliges . . . prowling around the back alleys of Savannah in the morning with his all-seeing camera . . . the Dos Passos of American photographers. We investigate bus stations, catch an old boy from the South with floppy Snopes hat waiting at Gate One of the station fingering a roadmap and saying "I dont know where this line go." *(The new Southern Aristocracy!* yell my friends seeing this picture.)

Night, and Florida, the lonely road night of snow white roadsigns at a wilderness crossing showing four endless unreadable nowhere directions, and the oncoming ghost cars. And the roadside gift shoppes of Florida by night, clay pelicans stuck in grass being a simple enough deal but not when photographed at night against the oncoming atom-ball headlights of a northbound car.

A trailer camp . . . a swimming pool . . . Spanish moss waving from old trees . . . and while prowling around to photograph a white pony tethered by the pool we spot four frogs on a stick floating in the cerulean pool . . . look closely and judge for yourself whether the frogs are meditating. A Melody Home trailer, the canaries in the window cage, and a little way down the road, the inevitable roadside Florida zoo and the old alligator slumbering like a thousand years and too lazy to shake his horny snout and shake off the peanut shells on his nose and eyes . . . mooning in his gravy. Other, grimmer trailer camps, like the one in Yukon Florida, the outboard motorboat on wheels, ready to go, the butane tank, the new lounge chair in the sun, the baby's canvas seat swing, the languorous pretty wife stepping out, cigarette in mouth . . . beyond her all wavy grass and swamps. . .

Now we're in Florida, we see the lady in the flowery print dress in a downtown Orlando Fla. drugstore looking over the flowery postcards on the rack, for now she's finally made it to Florida it's time to send postcards back to Newark.

Sunday, the road to Daytona Beach, the fraternity boys in the Ford with bare feet up on the dashboard, they love that car so much they even lie on top of it at the beach.

Americans, you cant separate them from their cars even at the most beautiful natural beach in the world, there they are taking lovely sunbaths practically under the oil pans of their perpetually new cars... The Wild Ones on their motorcycles, with T-shirt, boots, dark glasses, and ivy league slacks, the mad painting job on the motorcycle, and beyond, the confusion of cars by the waves. Another "wild one," not so wild, conversing politely from his motorcycle to a young family sprawled in the sand beside their car . . . in the background others leaning on car fenders. Critics of Mr. Frank's photography have asked "Why do you take so many pictures of cars?"

He answers, shrugging, "It's all I see everywhere . . . look for yourself."

Look for yourself, the soft day Atlantic waves washing in to the pearly flat hard sand, but everywhere you look, cars, fishtail Cadillacs, one young woman and a baby in the breeze to ten cars, or whole families under swung-across blankets from car to car camping in front of dreary motels.

The great ultimate shot of Mrs. Jones from Dubuque Iowa, come fifteen hundred miles just to turn her back to the very ocean and sit behind the open trunk of her husband's car (a car dealer), bored among blankets and spare tires.

A lesson for any writer . . . to follow a photographer and look at what he shoots . . . I mean a great photographer, an artist . . . and how he does it. The result: Whatever it is, it's America. It's the American Road and it awakens the eye every time.

The Great Western Bus Ride

Exhausting or not, there's no better way to see the West than
to take a good old bus and go batting along on regular roads
and come to all kinds of towns and cities where you can get
out and walk sometimes a whole hour and see the world and
come back to your bus and drive on. When I bought my ticket from San Francisco clear to New York City via the Pacific
Northwest the clerk thought I was crazy. I started back all
the way across the continent with my ten sandwiches and a
couple of dollars.

I slept through Sacramento Valley in the back of the bus
and woke up at seven a.m. in Redding with its white bunch-
grass hills at the end of empty streets. Then up through
Shasta Lake by Buckhorn and Hatchet Mountains, all great
Northwest timber and snow country that I enjoyed. Then
ghostly Mount Shasta in the distance; mountain lakes everywhere, high blue sky of mountain airs. A place called La
Moine, railroad shacks in valley flats. Across spectacular
mountains and timbered ridges to Dunsmuir, a little railroad
and lumber town, narrow ridge-town haunted above by
cloud-flirted Shasta of the walking snows. Terrible mount! —
with its ghost wraiths disporting in high blue day not even
waiting for the night.

The town of Weed. Well what'd he do up in Weed?
Nothing. Snow, cold, mountain pines, men on the porch of a
big inn facing empty spaces and the coal shuttles; grim deso-
late Weed, big lonely Black Butte right outside. After Weed
great clouds far off over the Cascade Ranges and Siskiyous of
Oregon, the clouds of the Oregon Trail. At Dorris, California,
intimations of ice caves far to the east down spatial snowy
corridors. Everything more joyous till at Klamath Falls in the

flats of the Klamath River I realized I was in an old-fashioned snowy, joyous American town and took a walk in the winy air. Little kids leaned on the bridge rail. Mills, red-brick alleys, businessmen on affairs in the sunny morning, bell-ringing, crisp, homelike town that made me homesick for my New York State. Up by great Klamath Lake rolling on the ridge of timber hills leading to east Oregon craters, wastes, rangelands and that mysteriously unknown junction of Oregon, Idaho and Nevada. The land of the Shasta Indians passed — the land of the Modocs now, Indians of the Lake, I saw some at Modoc Point and Agency Lake standing glumly by stores. We went up long, leisurely Sun Pass; saw a lake in a volcanic crater; and a pinpoint summit God wouldn't have dared sit on; everywhere great snowy rocks in the Northwest air, timber. Way back I saw the last of Mount Shasta that haunts poor Dunsmuir and poor Weed, a ghostly, shrouded, sneering mount. We climbed great Pengra Pass with its four feet of snow and big glorious redwoods clothed in snow — drooping, nodding, serried, gaunt, trimmed, orchestral in white, growing like ramrods on crooked cliffsides. Down to the Willamette Valley, a thin strip of poor farms haunted by distant volcanic craters in the dusk. This part of Oregon is a wilderness where people have to live in valleys like the upper Willamette and still be haunted as they milk sweet cows by those distant Encantadas of the blasted West . . . and then the snows melt in Pengra and the upper Willamette floods the cities of Eugene, Albany, Junction City, Oregon City, Salem, showing them who's so little in its beginning and showing up the sterile impotent volcanoes paralyzed in rage out there. Ah! — and then there's the Columbia River for floods, joined by the Willamette and the big Snake for the flooding of other cities.

Portland rose on the road; rain and snow as we crossed great dark Columbia over the bridge. Here too the river that once was the adventurous and commercial pulse of Portland was barred from the "public" by tug works, Naval bases, wire fences, just like the Mississippi in Algiers, Louisiana and I should have known before I took my walk. Chop suey joints of Portland on a Saturday night. I chose one on Broadway and sat among girl-and-boy dates, scribbling letters.

Now I was about to get to the source of the rainy night we cross on tidal highways, the snow North, the West that makes Mississippis: Montana! I looked forward to it mystified. Two hobo panhandlers in the back of the bus on the way out of Portland at midnight said they were bound for a place called The Dalles to beat a dollar, drunk. "Goddamit don't get us thrown off at Hood River!" complained the buddy.

"Aw hell I'm gonna beat the bus drahver for a couple!" We rolled in the big darkness of the Columbia River Valley in a blizzard. I could see big trees, bluffs, terrifying darknesses and the lights of Vancouver and Cape Horn across the shrouded waters. I had a chat with the wild bum. "My originator is Kansas City, Jackson County," he said, and "my place of origination is Texas" — or Bakersfield, or Modesto, or Delano, he couldn't make up his mind which lie was most suitable. He said he would be an old-time outlaw if J. Edgar Hoover hadn't made it against the law to steal. He said he was going to The Dalles to steal (a small farming and lumber town, he said) . . . on ahead out there in the frightful night's valley of the Columbia. I slept till two a.m. and woke up at Multnomah Falls and got out and stretched my legs. I couldn't altogether see in the eerie light, but a hooded white phantom was dropping water from his huge icy forehead. Hundreds of feet high from the rock bluff worn shelfwise by the patient frightful Columbia, from snow brows, the phantasmal waters from a mouth-like hole dropped and evaporated midways to mist. We were now on the floor of the valley looking up at ancient shores of rock and I could not see what

was in the darkness up and beyond that hood of ice, those
Falls — what hairy horrors? what craggy night? No stars.

The bus driver plunged along mad ridges all night. I slept
through Hood River, The Dalles, woke up briefly in the
morning to see Wallula in a mesa-like vast country of sagebrush and plains where the Columbia swung around to meet
the Snake and the Yakima. The brown plains of Pasco, and
on the horizon the misty long hills called Horse Heaven. I
had nothing to do but read the land; I was alone. Northeast
we went through Connell, Sprague, Cheney, through wheat
and cattle lands like east Wyoming, in a gale of blizzards to
Spokane, a snowy big town on a Sunday afternoon where
I plodded a mile to recover my black leather jacket at the
bus garage; I'd forgotten it. Then it was Idaho, great piny
snows of Fourth of July Pass; and Cataldo with its cluster of
houses homesteading in the wild mountain hole; nevertheless jovial faces, children playing, dogs barking, chimneys
smoking just like in Maine. In Mullan in the heart of immediate sheer slopes I thought of Jim Bridger and how, when
waking in the morning in the valley hole where Mullan now
stands, he looked ahead where the riverbed indisputably led
him across the vast crag lands he himself owned. Jim Bridger
didn't scramble up slopes as many of us do in civilization, he
followed his eternity of water beds and was satisfied. Jim
Bridger . . . grinding his coffee and slicing his bacon and frying his deer meat in the winter's shadow of the unknown
Bitterroot Mountains. What must he have thought back there
in the early nineteenth century, old squawman, solitary Jim
Bridger? These were my Montana-entry thoughts; it got dark
as we went up Lookout Pass in the Bitterroots. High in the
snowy grey we looked a mile below to the gulch where a single shack light burned. Two boys in a car almost went off the
ridge avoiding our bus, plumping instead into the plowed
snowbanks. When the driver went out to shovel them clear, in

the silence I opened my window to listen to the secret of the Bitterroots . . . a nameless hush. Down the pass we went to Deborgia, Montana, Frenchtown and Missoula. I began to see what Montana was like, at a wilderness way station there were ranchers, loggers and miners in the small bar in back playing cards and slot machines, outside it was the Montana night of bear and moose and wolf, pines, snow, secret rivers, the icy Bitterroots. One small light in the way station, in immensest dark, star-packed. I wondered what native young men thought of their Montana, what they'd thought in 1870, what the old men felt in it, and all the lovely women hidden. I slept en route to great Butte . . . over the Divide, near Anaconda and Pipestone Pass . . . Butte of the rough geographies.

Arriving, I stored my bag in a locker while some young Indian cat asked me to go drinking with him; he looked too crazy. I walked the sloping streets in super below-zero weather with my handkerchief tied tight around my leather collar and saw that everybody in Butte was drunk. It was Sunday night, I had hoped the saloons would stay open long enough for me to see them. They never even closed. In a great old-time saloon I had a giant beer. On the wall was a big electric signboard flashing gambling numbers. The bartender gave me the honor of selecting a number for him on the chance of beginner's luck. No soap. "Arrived here twenty-two years ago and stayed. Montanans drink too much, fight too much, love too much." What characters in there: old prospectors, gamblers, whores, miners, Indians, cowboys, tobacco-chewing businessmen! Groups of sullen Indians drank red rotgut in the john. Hundreds of men played cards in an atmosphere of smoke and spittoons. It was the end of my quest for an ideal bar. An old blackjack dealer tore my heart out, he reminded me so much of W. C. Fields and my father, fat, with a bulbous nose, great rugged pockmarked angelic face, wiping himself with a back-pocket handkerchief, green eyeshade, wheezing with big asthmatic laborious sadness in the Butte winter night games till he finally packed off for home and a snort to sleep another day. I also saw a ninety-year-old man called Old John who coolly played cards till dawn with slitted eyes, and had been doing so since 1880 in Montana . . . since the days of the winter cattle drive to Texas, and the days of Sitting Bull. There was another old man with an aged, loving, shaggy sheepdog who ankled off in the cold mountain night after satisfying his soul at cards. There were Greeks and Chinamen. The bus didn't leave Butte till dawn. I promised myself I'd come back. The bus roared down the slope and looking back I saw Butte on her fabled Gold Hill still lit like jewelry and sparkling on the mountainside in the blue northern dawn.

Across wild rocks and sagebrush to Three Forks, the source of everything, where the Madison and the Gallatin and the Jefferson Rivers in strange confluence act to form the cradle and beginnings of the Father of Waters, the unknown suckling place of the Mississippi River, the gargantuan secret of America that now in midwinter lay flooded and frozen in cakey inundations over vast acres of ranchland, covered with snow — hint of lush floods to come in the Natchez cobblestones a thousand miles away, hint of loamy plantations doomed to crumble far around the trail of the northwinged Missouri and old south-plunging Mississippi. This was where it all started, and it started in ice. Somewhere along the line a few miles down from old Three Forks elemental lightning cracks a tree one night and that log meanders restlessly, floating downstream; to Helena, Cascade, Wolf Point, Mandan of the winter snows, Council Bluffs; till above St. Louis where the male Missouri rushes huge muddy floods into the feminine Miss, this Odyssiac log from lonely Montana is carried by wide night-shores to Cairo; there to be joined by twigs from New York State via the Ohio and the Allegheny; and on down, a riven wandering log all water-heavy and sunken and turning over, coming in a wraith of mist and fogshrouds to bump that ferry that plows the brown water from Algiers to New Orleans; all the way thousands of miles from snowdrift to weeping willow till one with the movement of the night and the secret of sleep it floats around the keys where the oceangoing ship like an eternal ferry passes again its strange destiny, and goes out to the Gulf, out to night, sea, eternity, stars. A twig from my home and a log from far Montana — for the rain is the sea coming back, and the river (no lake) is the rain repassing to sea, draining a part of us, always a part of us; and the log rolls restlessly in the night, and never comes back.

In Big Timber, Montana, in a ramshackle old inn I saw a young cowboy who'd lost an arm in the war sitting with the old men around the stove looking with longing eyes at the boys loping by outside in the great Yellowstone snows . . . sad, unable to work for the rest of his life, protected by the old men of Montana, but *home* more than I could say with all my arms. Billings . . . Miles City . . . saddle stores . . . old bars. A man in an ornate vest, tired of cards, rose from a table underneath old photos of ranchers and elk antlers and went to the bar to eat a thick juicy steak. His wife and pretty daughter came in, ate with him. His sons all decked in new boots came in from the cold in Montana sheepskin coats, and they ate too. Then they packed things in the car and all drove back to the ranch house in the Yellowstone Valley in a grove of cottonwoods, a single light in the bleak wastes. The bus rolled on, to Terry, then Glendive, the last Montana way station; soon we were in Beach, North Dakota, in a dismal, bitter night beneath the cold moon. At Medora the incalculable Missouri's little tributary namesake had worn a rock canyon of ghostly snow rocks and buttes that stood in bulging haunted shapes in endlessness, and this was the heart of the Badlands, ambiguous heaths for the ghosts of old outlaws in flight from the law of raw towns. Such a town was Belfield. Then to Dickinson where the mad bus driver almost went off the road on a sudden snowdrift. It didn't bother him in the least, he bowled right along at seventy; a mile out of Dickinson he rammed into an impassable drift and there we stuck in the middle of a blizzard traffic jam. Suddenly there were many flashlights, sheepskinned men with shovels, confusion in the howling winds. Another Greyhound bus eastbound was stuck; a truck; many cars; major cause of the congestion was a small panel truck carrying slot machines to Butte, Montana. Whole crews of eager boys in red baseball caps and boots and jackets came rushing with shovels from nearby Dickinson, led by the energetic young sheriff. Their mothers waited at home with hot coffee. It was thirty below. The town of Dickinson took it upon itself to clear the emergency. When they made a hole in the snow, forlorn swirls came from the plain of Saskatchewan and filled it again. The maniacal bus driver decided to pile through. He backed from the snowdrift, gunned his diesel motor, yelled "Lookout!" out the window and took off on dry ground at fifty miles an hour and swoshed in. We swerved into the panel truck and hit the jackpot. We sideswiped a brand new Ford. We sloughed right through and came out the other side triumphant. There were cheers in the arctic night. It was just like a show. In Dickinson the café was crowded and full of late-night excitement. On the walls were photos of old-time ranchers and famous outlaws of the local past. The Dickinson boys of a less robust breed than the sheriff's boys played a homey pool in the back room — Badlands hipsters. Pretty girls sat wide-eyed with their families. Men came in from the howling midnight with news of more troubles on the road. The rotary snowplow had gone and hit the new Ford and sent the whole back end scattering and sowing in a thousand pieces over the plain of desolation. "Reckon any new Fords'll

grow out there come spring?" On the other side of town we
got stuck again behind a trailer truck. Boys hauled chains and
chipped ice and shouted in the gale. Us city slickers in the
bus that said CHICAGO on it watched with amazement, for
what would cause despair to the pasty characters of the East
was joy to the boys of the West. Near Fargo the back machin-
ery of the bus blew up and burned; we were stalled; the bus
froze and the passengers had to get out and spend the night
waiting in a diner. Nobody found me, I was flat on my back
in the backseat sleeping in pleasant dreams of Dakota in
June. Peach times, when summer's face I'd favor. I slept
through the repairs in the Fargo garage; the mechanics didn't
even bother me. Woke up refreshed, heard the news,
laughed, and we rolled into snowy Minnesota of farms and
church steeples; the end of the West, of troubles and raw
hopes, everything decided, satisfied here.

At St. Cloud, Minnesota, great Father Mississippi flowed
in a deep rocky bed beneath great valley skies with hints of
Mille Lacs and Rainy River to the north. Minneapolis, nothing but a sprawling dark city shooting off white communities
in the monotonous flat. Ah me, Montana, it was all over.
Night across the river darknesses and flat pinelands of
Wisconsin took us at dawn to the scraggly streets of Chicago
where workmen waited for buses, coughing. Old Eastern sadness returned to me.

But I had seen the West.

The Rumbling, Rambling Blues

I had been working in the railroad diner in Des Moines about five months when one night an old Negro hobo came to my counter.

He was an old *southern* Negro hobo and he came from those swamps. I was curious about the story of his life but he wouldn't talk about himself, just sang. In his pockmarked black skin, all white bristles, there gleamed enormous eyes that had grown larger since he left home. The bayou was his home town, the world was madder to see, he had been around, all 48 states, Canada and Mexico several times. He scared me when he first came in — not all customers spend three hours in the dark watching from across the street, as he did before he slid the doors in an empty hour to join me in a spate of time.

He made a strange remark about my secretest thoughts, which were about leaving Des Moines because I'd been there too long, only I was short of money and kept hesitating.

"You settle down this town, native boy? Or is you just *goin'!*"

"You mean if I don't live here, no."

"And is you goin' someplace, or just goin'!" He showed me yellow teeth and wheezed a remanent laugh.

"No sir, Pop, I guess I'm just going." I said it too anxiously. He wrapped himself up in an evil old smile and didn't believe it.

Like the grimy white brakemen who came in to eat their gloomy meals, he was a man possessed of a suffering that was seamed into the flesh, face and neck; but who sang about it, made no bones; after all had suffered just a little more than they did, by a shade exactly; and whose suffering compared to mine was as the rings of an age-oak and the rings of a sapling tree. Worse, a thousand winters had caked his skin, and summers cracked it. Around him the fog was a palpable shroud; its cold, gray exhalations seemed to breathe about his mouth; so were it not for his warm eyes he would have shrove his songs and put a blanket round him. But he walked the American night just as he was: the burlap pants, the rope, and the shapeless tarpaulin apron, all greasy and dark like Beelzebub in hell, fit for every jail that gives no supper: and the saddest, best old bum of all old bums I've seen.

He had one lead nickel for a coffee. I picked at the chopped meat and rolled him a hamburger dinner, with the works, free. With this I gave him a strawberry shortcake I paid for on the sly. He said it was the best dinner he ever had and sat content.

He sat, or half-sat, at the very end of the counter, near the door, so no newcomer could accuse him of really frequenting the dining room, and if so, the door was his. From that position, which I did not quarrel for, he began singing like he knew I would really enjoy it and for his own reminiscive pleasures. His songs were those mysterious rumbling, rambling blues that you hear with low-register guitar and unknown words rising out of the Deep South night like a groan, like a fire beyond the trees. He pronounced his words so darkly I had to ask him what they meant: "nine-tunny-na," that was nineteen twenty nine, "polan-may" was Portland, Maine, "tunsee" Tennessee, so on. Print can't read like he sounded, so mournful, hoarse and swampy-like. He started with a record of what evidently was his youth.

> *Left Louisiana*
> *Nineteen twenty nine*
> *To go along the river*
> *'Thout a daddy-blame dime.*

Up old Montana
In the cold, cold Fall
I found my father
In a gam-balin hall.

Father, father,
Wherever you been?
Unloved is lost
When you so blame small.

Dear son, he said,
Don't a-worry 'bout me,
I'm 'bout to die
Of the misery.

Went south together
In an old freight train
Night my father died
In the cold, cold rain.

I counted the years and figured he left home for the first time when he was almost 30, to go look for his father up the river, and he said that was so, adding, pointing, "He was *way* up that river, yander Big Muddy go."

Then he sang the general lament of his life and I died to hear it.

Been to Butte Montana
Been to Portland Maine
Been to San Francisco
Been in all the rain
Lord, Lord,
I never found no li'l girl.

Cross the Brazos river
Cross the Tennessee
Cross the Niobrara
Cross the Jordan sea
Lord, Lord,
I never found no li'l girl.

Home in Opelousas
Home in Wounded Knee
Home in Ogallala
Home I'll never be
Lord, Lord,
I never found no li'l girl.

He suddenly said to me, "Slim, you's a river log ain't rolling."

"What do you mean?"

He only said he had a song for me that nobody had ever heard except a few witch doctors and himself. "Witch doctor sing this when he feel sad and gotsa leave the bayou. It's a sign." He grunted.

Down — yum — down
Down — yum — down
Roll — faw — log
Roll — faw — log
Well — tha — snake
Well — tha — snake
    LOOKAT!

He whistled shrilly through his teeth, and smiled to show the song was over. Suddenly his gnarled finger was pointed at me in advice. "In N'awleans the log roll faw way from the top-big-muddy that ain't got CAUGHT in a snag where witch doctor lie down with the snake."

I understood those logs he was talking about — I had seen them from the decks of ships in New Orleans at night, wandering logs all riven, water-heavy, sunken and turning over that come with the Missouri rushing hugely into the floods of the Mississippi all the way from top-big-muddy, which is lonely old Montana in the North, Odyssiac logs, stately wanderers, moving slowly with satisfaction and eternity down wide night shores out to sea — but I never knew what he meant about the witch doctor and the snake. He wheezed that laugh.

It was a prophetic night for me. I watched him go across the railyards — said he was going to "Sanacisca" right soon, or "Awg'n," which are San Francisco and Ogden, in Utah, I know — a tarpaulin ghost aimed for the nearest empties on the track, to fold inside the dryest reefers or find his bed of paper, in any old gondola, any box, even the rushing cold rods themselves, "Just long as they ball that jack!" as he yelled when he left. So he was gone.

In the morning I collected my pay, packed my old torn bag, and rode a bus to the edge of town. I'd never get caught, I'd roll far too. I got on that old road again. I knew I would see him somewhere at least once more.

On the Beats

Aftermath: The Philosophy of the Beat Generation

The Beat Generation, that was a vision that we had, John Clellon Holmes and I, and Allen Ginsberg in an even wilder way, in the late Forties, of a generation of crazy illuminated hipsters suddenly rising and roaming America, serious, curious, bumming and hitchhiking everywhere, ragged, beatific, beautiful in an ugly graceful new way — a vision gleaned from the way we had heard the word *beat* spoken on street corners on Times Square and in the Village, in other cities in the downtown-city-night of postwar America — *beat*, meaning down and out but full of intense conviction. We'd even heard old 1910 Daddy Hipsters of the streets speak the word that way, with a melancholy sneer. It never meant juvenile delinquents; it meant characters of a special spirituality who didn't gang up but were solitary Bartlebies staring out the dead wall window of our civilization. The subterranean heroes who'd finally turned from the "freedom" machine of the West and were taking drugs, digging bop, having flashes of insight, experiencing the "derangement of the senses," talking strange, being poor and glad, prophesying a new style for American culture, a new style (we thought) completely free from European influences (unlike the Lost Generation), a new incantation. The same thing was almost going on in the postwar France of Sartre and Genet and what's more we knew about it. But as to the actual existence of a Beat Generation, chances are it was really just an idea in our minds. We'd stay up twenty-four hours drinking cup after cup of black coffee, playing record after record of Wardell Gray, Lester Young, Dexter Gordon, Willis Jackson, Lennie Tristano and all the rest, talking madly about that holy new feeling out there in the streets. We'd write stories about some strange beatific Negro hepcat saint with goatee hitchhiking across Iowa with taped-up horn bringing the secret message of *blowing* to other coasts, other cities, like a veritable Walter the Penniless leading an invisible First Crusade. We had our mystic heroes and wrote, nay sung novels about them, erected long poems celebrating the new "angels" of the American underground. In actuality there was only a handful of real hip swinging cats and what there was vanished mighty swiftly during the Korean War when (and after) a sinister new kind of efficiency appeared in America; maybe it was the result of the universalization of television and nothing else (the Polite Total Police Control of Dragnet's "peace" officers), but the beat characters after 1950 vanished into jails and madhouses, or were shamed into silent conformity; the generation itself was short-lived and small in number.

But there'd be no sense in writing this if it weren't equally true that, by some miracle of metamorphosis, suddenly the Korean postwar youth emerged cool and beat, had picked up the gestures and the style; soon it was everywhere, the new look, the "twisted" slouchy look; finally it began to appear even in movies (James Dean) and on television; bop arrangements that were once the secret ecstasy music of beat contemplatives began to appear in every pit in every square orchestra book (cf. the works of Neal Hefti and not meaning Basie's book), the bop visions became common property of the commercial, popular, cultural world; the use of expressions like "crazy," "hungup," "hassle," "make it," "like" ("like make it over sometime, like"), "go," became familiar and common usage; the ingestion of drugs became official (tranquilizers and the rest); and even the clothes style of the beat hipsters carried over to the new rock 'n' roll youth via Montgomery Clift (leather jacket), Marlon Brando (T-shirt) and Elvis Presley (long sideburns), and the Beat Generation, though dead, was resurrected and justified.

It really happened, and the sad thing is, that while I am asked to explain the Beat Generation, there is no actual original Beat Generation left.

As to an analysis of what it means . . . who knows? Even in this late stage of civilization when money is the only thing that really matters to *everybody*, I think perhaps it is the Second Religiousness that Oswald Spengler prophesied for the West (in America the final home of Faust), because there are elements of hidden religious significance in the way, for instance, that a guy like Stan Getz, the highest jazz genius of his "beat" generation, when put in jail for trying to hold up a drugstore, suddenly had visions of God and repented. Strange talk we'd heard among the early hipsters of "the end of the world" at the "second coming," of "stoned-out visions" and even visitations, all *believing*, all inspired and fervent and free of Bourgeois-Bohemian Materialism.

One kid had geekish visions of Armageddon (experienced in Sing Sing); another, visions of reincarnation under God's will. Still another, strange visions of Texas Apocalypse (before and after the Texas City explosion). Then there was one boy's mad attempt to claim asylum in a church (cops broke his arm getting him out), and one Times Square kid's vision of the Second Coming being televised (all taking place, a definite fact, in the midst of everyday contemporary life in the minds of typical members of my generation whom I know); reappearances of the early Gothic springtime feeling of Western mankind before it went on its 'Civilization' Rationale and developed relativity, jets and superbombs had supercolassal, bureaucratic, totalitarian, benevolent, Big Brother structures. So, as Spengler says, when comes the sunset of our culture (due now, according to his morphological graphs) and the dust of civilized striving settles, lo, the clear, late-day glow reveals the original concerns again, reveals a *beatific* indifference to things that are Caesar's, for instance, a tiredness of that, and a yearning for, a regret for, the transcendant value, or "God," again, "Heaven" the spiritual regret for Endless Love which our theory of electromagnetic gravitation, our conquest of space will prove, and instead of only *techniques of efficiency,* all will be left, as with a population that has gone through a violent earthquake, will be the Last Things . . . again.

We all know about the Religious Revival, Billy Graham and all, which the Beat Generation, even the Existentialists with all their intellectual overlays and pretenses of indifference, represent an even deeper religiousness, the desire to be gone, out of this world (which is not our kingdom), "high," ecstatic, saved, as if the visions of the cloistral saints of Chartres and Clairvaux were back with us again bursting like weeds through the sidewalks of stiffened civilization wearying through its late motions.

Or maybe the Beat Generation, which is the offspring of the Lost Generation, is just another step toward that last, pale generation which will not know the answers either.

In any case, indications are that its effect has taken root in American culture.

Maybe.

Or, what difference does it make?

Lamb, No Lion

The Beat Generation is no hoodlumism. As the man who suddenly thought of that word "beat" to describe our generation, I would like to have my little say about it before everyone else in the writing field begins to call it "roughneck," "violent," "heedless," "rootless." How can *people* be rootless? Heedless of what? Wants? Roughneck because you don't come on elegant?

Beat doesn't mean tired, or bushed, so much as it means *beato*, the Italian for beatific: to be in a state of beatitude, like St. Francis, trying to love all life, trying to be utterly sincere with everyone, practicing endurance, kindness, cultivating joy of heart. How can this be done in our mad modern world of multiplicities and millions? By practicing a little solitude, going off by yourself once in a while to store up that most precious of golds: the vibrations of sincerity.

Being bugged is not being beat. You may be withdrawn, but you don't have to be mean about it. Beatness is not a form of tired old criticism. It is a form of spontaneous affirmation. What kinda culture you gonna have with everybody's gray faces saying "I don't think that's quite correct"?

Let's start at the beginning. After publishing my book about the beat generation I was asked to explain beatness on TV, on radio, by people everywhere. They were all under the impression that being beat was just a lot of frantic nowhere hysteria. What are you searching for? they asked me. I answered that I was waiting for God to show his face. (Later I got a letter from a 16-year-old girl saying that was exactly what she'd been waiting for too.) They asked: How could this have anything to do with mad hepcats? I answered that even mad happy hepcats with all their kicks and chicks and hep talk were creatures of God laid out here in this infinite universe without knowing what for. And besides I have never heard more talk about God, the Last Things, the soul, the where-we-going than among the kids of my generation: and not the intellectual kids alone, *all* of them. In the faces of my questioners was the hopeless question: But Why? Billy Graham has a half a million spiritual babies. This generation has many more "beat kiddies," and the relationship is close.

The Lost Generation of the 20s believed in nothing so they went their rather cynical way putting everything down. That generation forms the corpus of our authority today, and is looking with disfavor upon us, under beetling brows, at us who want to *swing* — in life, in art, in everything, in the confession of everything to everyone. The Lost Generation put it down; the Beat Generation is picking it all up again. The Beat Generation *believes* that there will be some justification for all the horror of life. The first of the Four Noble Truths is: All Life Is Suffering. Yet I hear them talk about how it's worth it, if you only *believed*, if you let that holy flow gush endlessly out of that secret source of living bliss.

"Man, I dig everything!" So many cats said that to me on the sidewalks of the 1940s, when beatness rose like an ethereal flower out of the squalor and madness of the times. "But why?" I'd say. "You haven't got a cent, no place to sleep." Answer: "Man, you gotta stay high, that's all." Then I'd see these same characters next day all bushed and beat brooding on a bench in the park, refusing to talk to anybody, *storing* up for more belief.

And there they all were, at night, the bop musicians were on the stand blowing, the beat was great, you'd see hundreds of heads nodding in the smoky dimness, nodding to the music, "Yes, yes, yes" is what their nodding heads said, so musingly, so prettily, so *mystically*. Musicians waiting for their turn to take a solo also listened nodding, Yes. I saw a whole generation nodding yes. (I also saw the junkies nod No over their bed-edges.)

I don't think the Beat Generation is going to be a moronic band of dope addicts and hoodlums. My favorite beat buddies were all *kind*, good kids, eager, sincere ("Now lend me five minutes of your time and listen to *every word* I'm going to say!") . . . such tender concern! Such a pathetic human hope that all will be communicated and received, and all made well by this mysterious union of minds. The dope thing will die out. That was a fad, like bathtub gin. In the Beat Generation instead of an old Lost Generation champagne bottle intertwined in one silk stocking, you found an old benny tube in the closet, or an ancient roach in a dresser, all covered with dust. The dope thing was confined to a handful of medical metabolic junkies before it was given such publicity by the authorities. Then it got out of hand.

As to sex, why not? One woman interviewer asked me if I thought sexual passion was messy, I said, "No, it's the gateway to paradise."

Only bitter people put down life. The Beat Generation is going to be a sweetie (as the great Pinky Lee would say, Lee who loves children, and all generations are children).

I only hope there won't be a war to hurt all these beautiful people, and I don't think there will be. There appears to be a Beat Generation all over the world, even behind the Iron Curtain. I think Russia wants a share of what America has — food and clothing and pleasantries for most everyone.

I prophesy that the Beat Generation which is supposed to be nutty nihilism in the guise of new hipness, is going to be the most sensitive generation in the history of America and therefore it can't help but do good. Whatever wrong comes will come out of evil interference. If there is any quality that I have noticed more strongly than anything else in this generation, it is the spirit of non-interference with the lives of others. I had a dream that I didn't want the lion to eat the lamb and the lion came up and lapped my face like a big puppy dog and then I picked up the lamb and it kissed me. This is the dream of the Beat Generation.

The Origins of the Beat Generation

This necessarily'll have to be about myself. I'm going all out.

That nutty picture of me on the cover of *On the Road* results from the fact that I had just gotten down from a high mountain where I'd been for two months completely alone and usually I was in the habit of combing my hair of course because you have to get rides on the highway and all that and you usually want girls to look at you as though you were a man and not a wild beast but my poet friend Gregory Corso opened his shirt and took out a silver crucifix that was hanging from a chain and said "Wear this and wear it outside your shirt and don't comb your hair!" so I spent several days around San Francisco going around with him and others like that, to parties, arties, parts, jam sessions, bars, poetry readings, churches, walking talking poetry in the streets, walking talking God in the streets (and at one point a strange gang of hoodlums got mad and said "What right does he got to wear that?" and my own gang of musicians and poets told them to cool it) and finally on the third day *Mademoiselle* magazine wanted to take pictures of us all so I posed just like that, wild hair, crucifix, and all, with Gregory Corso, Allen Ginsberg and Phil Whalen, and the only publication which later did not erase the crucifix from my breast (from that plaid sleeveless cotton shirt-front) was *The New York Times*, therefore *The New York Times* is as beat as I am, and I'm glad I've got a friend. I mean it sincerely, God bless *The New York Times* for not erasing the crucifix from my picture as though it was something distasteful. As a matter of fact, who's *really* beat around here, I mean if you wanta talk of Beat as "beat down" the people who erased the crucifix are really the "beat down" ones and not *The New York Times*, myself, and Gregory Corso the poet. I am not ashamed to wear the crucifix of my Lord. It is because I am Beat, that is, I believe in beatitude and that God so loved the world that he gave his only begotten son to it. I am sure no priest would've condemned me for wearing the crucifix outside my shirt everywhere and *no matter where* I went, even to have my picture taken by *Mademoiselle.* So you people don't believe in God. So you're all big smart know-it-all Marxists and Freudians, hey? Why don't you come back in a million years and tell me all about it, angels?

Recently Ben Hecht said to me on TV "Why are you afraid to speak out your mind, what's wrong with this country, what is everybody afraid of?" Was he talking to me? And all he wanted me to do was speak out my mind *against* people, he sneeringly brought up Dulles, Eisenhower, the Pope, all kinds of people like that habitually he would sneer at with Drew Pearson, *against* the world he wanted, this is his idea of freedom, he calls it freedom. Who knows, my God, but that the universe is not one vast sea of compassion actually, the veritable holy honey, beneath all this show of personality and cruelty. In fact who knows but that it isn't the solitude of the oneness of the essence of everything, the solitude of the actual oneness of the unbornness of the unborn essence of everything, nay the true pure foreverhood, that big blank potential that can ray forth anything it wants from its pure store, that blazing bliss, *Mattivajrakaruna* the Transcendental Diamond Compassion! No, I want to speak *for* things, for the crucifix I speak out, for the Star of Israel I speak out, for the divinest man who ever lived who was a German (Bach) I speak out, for sweet Mohammed I speak out, for Buddha I speak out, for Lao-tse and Chuang-tse I speak out, for D. T. Suzuki I speak out . . . why should I attack what I love out of life. This is Beat. Live your lives out? Naw, *love* your lives out. When they come and stone you at least you won't have a glass house, just your glassy flesh.

That wild eager picture of me on the cover of *On the Road* where I look so Beat goes back much further than 1948 when John Clellon Holmes (author of *Go* and *The Horn*) and I were sitting around trying to think up the meaning of the Lost Generation and the subsequent Existentialism and I said "You know, this is really a beat generation" and he leapt up and said "That's it, that's right!" It goes back to the 1880's when my grandfather Jean-Baptiste Kerouac used to go out on the porch in big thunderstorms and swing his kerosene lamp at the lightning and yell "Go ahead, go, if you're more powerful than I am strike me and put the light out!" while the mother and the children cowered in the kitchen. And the light never went out. Maybe since I'm supposed to be the spokesman of the Beat Generation (I *am* the originator of the term, and around it the term and the generation have taken shape) it should be pointed out that all this "Beat" guts therefore goes back to my ancestors who were Bretons who were the most independent group of nobles in all old Europe and kept fighting Latin France to the last wall (although a big blond bosun on a merchant ship snorted when I told him my ancestors were Bretons in Cornwall, Brittany, "Why, we Wikings used to swoop down and steal your nets!"). Breton, Wiking, Irishman, Indian, madboy, it doesn't make any difference, there is no doubt about the Beat Generation, at least the core of it, being a swinging group of new American men intent on joy. . . . Irresponsibility? Who wouldn't help a dying man on an empty road? No and the Beat Generation goes back to the wild parties my father used to have at home in the 1920's and 1930's in New England that were so fantastically loud nobody could sleep for blocks around and when the cops came they always had a drink. It goes back to the wild and raving childhood of playing the Shadow under windswept trees of New England's gleeful autumn, and the howl of the

Moon Man on the sandbank until we caught him in a tree (he was an "older" guy of 15), the maniacal laugh of certain neighbourhood madboys, the furious humour of whole gangs playing basketball till long after dark in the park, it goes back to those crazy days before World War II when teenagers drank beer on Friday nights at Lake ballrooms and worked off their hangovers playing baseball on Saturday afternoon followed by a dive in the brook — and our fathers wore straw hats like W.C. Fields. It goes back to the completely senseless babble of the Three Stooges, the ravings of the Marx Brothers (the tenderness of Angel Harpo at harp, too).

It goes back to the inky ditties of old cartoons (Krazy Kat with the irrational brick) — to Laurel and Hardy in the Foreign Legion — to Count Dracula and his *smile* to Count Dracula shivering and hissing back before the Cross — to the Golem horrifying the persecutors of the Ghetto — to the quiet sage in a movie about India, unconcerned about the plot — to the giggling old Tao Chinaman trotting down the sidewalk of old Clark Gable Shanghai — to the holy old Arab warning the hotbloods that Ramadan is near. To the Werewolf of London a distinguished doctor in his velour smoking jacket smoking his pipe over a lamplit tome on botany and suddenly hairs grown on his hands, his cat hisses, and he slips out into the night with a cape and a slanty cap like the caps of people in breadlines — to Lamont Cranston so cool and sure suddenly becoming the frantic Shadow going mwee hee hee ha ha in the alleys of New York imagination. To Popeye the sailor and the Sea Hag and the meaty gunwales of boats, to Cap'n Easy and Wash Tubbs screaming with ecstasy over canned peaches on a cannibal isle, to Wimpy looking X-eyed for a juicy hamburger such as they make no more. To Jiggs ducking before a household of furniture flying through the air, to Jiggs and the boys at the bar and the corned beef and cabbage of old woodfence noons —

to King Kong his eyes looking into the hotel window with tender huge love for Fay Wray — nay, to Bruce Cabot in mate's cap leaning over the rail of a fogbound ship saying "Come aboard." It goes back to when grapefruits were thrown at crooners and harvestworkers at bar-rails slapped burlesque queens on the rump. To when fathers took their sons to the Twi League game. To the days of Babe Callahan on the waterfront, Dick Barthelmess camping under a London streetlamp. To dear old Basil Rathbone looking for the Hound of the Baskervilles (a dog big as the Gray Wolf who will destroy Odin) — to dear old bleary Doctor Watson with a brandy in his hand. To Joan Crawford her raw shanks in the fog, in striped blouse smoking a cigarette at sticky lips in the door of the waterfront dive. To train whistles of steam engines out above the moony pines. To Maw and Paw in the Model A clanking on to get a job in California selling used cars making a whole lotta money. To the glee of America, the honesty of America, the honesty of oldtime grafters in straw hats as well as the honesty of oldtime waiters in line at the Brooklyn Bridge in *Winterset*, the funny spitelessness of old big-fisted America like big Boy Williams saying "Hoo? Hee? Huh?" in a movie about Mack Trucks and slidingdoor lunchcarts. To Clark Gable, his certain smile, his confident leer. Like my grandfather this America was invested with wild selfbelieving individuality and this had begun to disappear around the end of World War II with so many great guys dead (I can think of half a dozen from my own boyhood groups) when suddenly it began to emerge again, the hipsters began to appear gliding around saying "Crazy, man."

When I first saw the hipsters creeping around Times Square in 1944 I didn't like them either. One of them, Huncke of Chicago, came up to me and said "Man, I'm beat." I knew right away what he meant somehow. At that time I still didn't like bop which was then being introduced by Bird Parker and Dizzy Gillespie and Bags Jackson (on vibes), the last of the great swing musicians was Don Byas who went to Spain right after, but then I began . . . but earlier I'd dug all my jazz in the old Minton Playhouse (Lester Young, Ben Webster, Joey Guy, Charlie Christian, others) and when I first heard Bird and Diz in the Three Deuces I knew they were serious musicians playing a goofy new sound and didn't care what I thought, or what my friend Seymour thought. In fact I was leaning against the bar with a beer when Dizzy came over for a glass of water from the bartender, put himself right against me and reached both arms around both sides of my head to get the glass and danced away, as though knowing I'd be singing about him someday, or that one of his arrangements would be named after me someday by some goofy circumstance. Charlie Parker was spoken of in Harlem as the greatest new musician since Chu Berry and Louis Armstrong.

Anyway, the hipsters, whose music was bop, they looked like criminals but they kept talking about the same things I liked, long outlines of personal experience and vision, night-long confessions full of hope that had become illicit and repressed by War, stirrings, rumblings of a new soul (that same old human soul). And so Huncke appeared to us and said "I'm beat" with radiant light shining out of his despairing eyes . . . a word perhaps brought from some midwest carnival or junk cafeteria. It was a new language, actually spade (Negro) jargon but you soon learned it, like "hung up" couldn't be a more economical term to mean so many things. Some of these hipsters were raving mad and talked continually. It was jazzy. Symphony Sid's all-night modern jazz and bop show was always on. By 1948 it began to take shape. That was a wild vibrating year when a group of us would walk down the street and yell hello and even stop and talk to anybody that gave us a friendly look. The hipsters had eyes. That was the year I saw Montgomery Clift, unshaven, wearing a sloppy jacket, slouching down Madison Avenue with a companion. It was the year I saw Charley Bird Parker strolling down Eighth Avenue in a black turtleneck sweater with Babs Gonzales and a beautiful girl.

By 1948 the hipsters, or beatsters, were divided into cool and hot. Much of the misunderstanding about hipsters and the Beat Generation in general today derives from the fact that there are two distinct styles of hipsterism: the "cool" today is your bearded laconic sage, or schlerm, before a hardly touched beer in a beatnik dive, whose speech is low and unfriendly, whose girls say nothing and wear black; the "hot" today is the crazy talkative shining eyed (often innocent and openhearted) nut who runs from bar to bar, pad to pad looking for everybody, shouting, restless, lushy, trying to "make it" with the subterranean beatniks who ignore him. Most Beat Generation artists belong to the hot school, naturally since that hard gemlike flame needs a little heat. In many cases the mixture is 50-50. It was a hot hipster like myself who finally cooled it in Buddhist meditation, though when I go in a jazz joint I still feel like yelling "Blow baby blow!" to the musicians though nowadays I'd get 86'd for this. In 1948 the "hot hipsters" were racing around in cars like in *On the Road* looking for wild bawling jazz like Willis Jackson or Lucky Thompson (the early) or Chubby Jackson's big band while the "cool hipsters" cooled it in dead silence before formal and excellent musical groups like Lennie Tristano or Miles Davis. It's still just about the same, except that it has begun to grow into a national generation and the name "Beat" has stuck (though all hipsters hate the word).

The word "beat" originally meant poor, down and out, deadbeat, on the bum, sad, sleeping in subways. Now that the word is belonging officially it is being made to stretch to include people who do not sleep in subways but have a certain new gesture, or attitude, which I can only describe as a new *more*. "Beat Generation" has simply become the slogan or label for a revolution in manners in America. Marlon Brando was not really first to portray it on the screen. Dane Clark with his pinched Dostoievskyan face and Brooklyn accent, and of course Garfield, were first. The private eyes were Beat, if you will recall. Bogart. Lorre was Beat. In *M*, Peter Lorre started a whole revival, I mean the slouchy street walk.

I wrote *On the Road* in three weeks in the beautiful month of May 1951 while living in the Chelsea district of lower West Side Manhattan, on a 100-foot roll and put the Beat Generation in words in there, saying at the point where I am taking part in a wild kind of collegiate party with a bunch of kids in an abandoned miner's shack "These kids are great but where are Dean Moriarty and Carlo Marx? Oh well I guess they wouldn't belong in this gang, they're too *dark*, too strange, too suberannean and I am slowly beginning to join a new kind of *beat* generation." The manuscript of *Road* was turned down on the grounds that it would displease the sales manager of my publisher at that time, though the editor, a very intelligent man, said "Jack this is just like Dostoievsky, but what can I do at this time?" It was too early. So for the next six years I was a bum, a brakeman, a seaman, a panhandler, a pseudo-Indian in Mexico, anything and everything, and went on writing because my hero was Goethe and I believed in art and hoped some day to write the third part of *Faust*, which I have done in *Doctor Sax*. Then in 1952 an article was published in *The New York Times* Sunday magazine saying, the headline, "'This is a Beat Generation'" (in quotes like that) and in the article it said that I had come up with the term first "when the face was harder to recognise," the face of the generation. After that there was some talk of the Beat Generation but in 1955 I published an excerpt from *Road* (melling it with parts of *Visions of Neal*) under the pseudonym "Jean-Louis," it was entitled *Jazz of the Beat Generation* and was copyrighted as being an excerpt from a novel-in-progress entitled *Beat Generation* (which I later changed to *On the Road* at the insistence of my new editor) and so then the term moved a little faster. The term and the cats. Everywhere began to appear strange hepcats and even college kids went around hep and cool and using the terms I'd heard on Times Square in the early Forties, it was growing somehow. But when the publishers finally took a dare and published *On the Road* in 1957 it burst open, it mushroomed, everybody began yelling about a Beat Generation. I was being interviewed everywhere I went for "what I meant" by such a thing. People began to call themselves beatniks, beats, jazzniks, bopniks, bugniks and finally I was called the "avatar" of all this.

Yet it was as a Catholic, it was not at the insistence of any of these "niks" and certainly not with their approval either, that I went one afternoon to the church of my childhood (one of them), Ste. Jeanne d'Arc in Lowell, Mass., and suddenly with tears in my eyes and had a vision of what I must have really meant with "Beat" anyhow when I heard the holy silence in the church (I was the only one in there, it was five p.m., dogs were barking outside, children yelling, the fall leaves, the candles were flickering alone just for me), the vision of the word Beat as being to mean beatific. . . . There's the priest preaching on Sunday morning, all of a sudden through a side door of the church comes a group of Beat Generation characters in strapped raincoats like the I.R.A. coming in silently to "dig" the religion . . . I knew it then.

But this was 1954, so then what horror I felt in 1957 and

later 1958 naturally to suddenly see "Beat" being taken up by everybody, press and TV and Hollywood borscht circuit to include the "juvenile delinquency" shot and the horrors of a mad teeming billyclub New York and L.A. and they began to call *that* Beat, *that* beatific. . . . Bunch of fools marching against the San Francisco Giants protesting baseball, as if (now) in my name and I, my childhood ambition to be a big league baseball star hitter like Ted Williams so that when Bobby Thomson hit that homerun in 1951 I trembled with joy and couldn't get over it for days and wrote poems about how it is possible for the human spirit to win after all! Or, when a nurder, a routine murder took place in North Beach, they labelled it a Beat Generation slaying although in my childhood I'd been famous as an eccentric in my block for stopping the younger kids from throwing rocks at the squirrels, for stopping them from frying snakes in cans or trying to blow up frogs with straws. Because my brother had died at the age of nine, his name was Gerard Kerouac, and he'd told me "Ti Jean never hurt any living being, all living beings whether it's just a little cat or squirrel or whatever, all, are going to heaven straight into God's snowy arms so never hurt anything and if you see anybody hurt anything stop them as best you can" and when he died a file of gloomy nuns in black from St. Louis de France parish had filed (1926) to his deathbed to hear his last words about Heaven. And my father, too, Leo, had never lifted a hand to punish me, or to punish the little pets in our house, and this teaching was delivered to me by the men in my house and I have never had anything to do with violence, hatred, cruelty, and all that horrible nonsense which, nevertheless, because God is gracious beyond all human imagining, he will forgive in the long end . . . that million years I'm asking about you, America.

And so now they have beatnik routines on TV, starting with satires about girls in black and fellows in jeans with snapknives and sweatshirts and swastikas tattooed under their armpits, it will come to respectable m.c.s of spectaculars coming out nattily attired in Brooks Brothers jean-type tailoring and sweater-type pull-ons, in other words, it's a simple change in fashion and manners, just a history crust — like from the Age of Reason, from old Voltaire in a chair to romantic Chatterton in the moonlight — from Teddy Roosevelt to Scott Fitzgerald . . . so there's nothing to get excited about. Beat comes out, actually, of old American whoopee and it will only change a few dresses and pants and make chairs useless in the livingroom and pretty soon we'll have Beat Secretaries of State and there will be instituted new tinsels, in fact new reasons for malice and new reasons for virtue and new reasons for forgiveness. . . .

But yet, but yet, woe, woe unto those who think that the Beat Generation means crime, delinquency, immorality, amorality . . . woe unto those who attack it on the grounds that they simply don't understand history and the yearnings of human souls . . . woe unto those who don't realise that America must, will, is, changing now, for the better I say. Woe unto those who believe in the atom bomb, who believe in hating mothers and fathers, who deny the most important of the Ten Commandments, woe unto those (though) who don't believe in the unbelievable sweetness of sex love, woe unto those who are the standard bearers of death, woe unto those who believe in conflict and horror and violence and fill our books and screens and livingrooms with that crap, woe in fact unto those who make evil movies about the Beat Generation where innocent housewives are raped by beatniks! Woe unto those who are the real dreary sinners that even God finds room to forgive. . . .

Woe unto those who spit on the Beat Generation, the wind'll blow it back.

On Writing

Essentials of Spontaneous Prose

SET-UP. The object is set before the mind, either in reality, as in sketching (before a landscape or teacup or old face) or is set in the memory wherein it becomes the sketching from memory of a definite image-object.

PROCEDURE. Time being of the essence in the purity of speech, sketching language is undisturbed flow from the mind of personal secret idea-words, *blowing* (as per jazz musician) on subject of image.

METHOD. No periods separating sentence-structures already arbitrarily riddled by false colons and timid usually needless commas — but the vigorous space dash separating rhetorical breathing (as jazz musician drawing breath between outblown phrases) — "measured pauses which are the essentials of our speech" — "divisions of the *sounds* we hear" — "time and how to note it down."

SCOPING. Not "selectivity" of expression but following free deviation (association) of mind into limitless blow-on-subject seas of thought, swimming in sea of English with no discipline other than rhythms of rhetorical exhalation and expostulated statement, like a fist coming down on a table with each complete utterance, bang! (the spacedash) — Blow as deep as you want — write as deeply, fish as far down as you want, satisfy yourself first, then reader cannot fail to receive telepathic shock and meaning-excitement by same laws operating in his own human mind.

LAG IN PRODUCERE. No pause to think of proper word but the infantile pileup of scatalogical buildup words till satisfaction is gained, which will turn out to be a great appending rhythm to a thought and be in accordance with Great Law of timing.

TIMING.   Nothing is muddy that *runs in time* and to laws of *time* — Shakespearian stress of dramatic need to speak now in own unalterable way or forever hold tongue — *no revisions* (except obvious rational mistakes, such as names or *calculated* insertions in act of not-writing but *inserting).*

CENTER OF INTEREST.   Begin not from preconceived idea of what to say about image but from jewel center of interest in subject of image at *moment* of writing, and write outwards swimming in sea of language to peripheral release and exhaustion — Do not afterthink except for poetic or P. S. reasons. Never afterthink to "improve" or defray impressions, as, the best writing is always the most painful personal wrung-out tossed from cradle warm protective mind — tap from yourself the song of yourself, *blow! — now! — your* way is your only way — "good" — or "bad" — always honest. ('ludicrous') spontaneous, 'confessional' interesting, because not 'crafted.' Craft *is* craft.

STRUCTURE OF WORK.   Modern bizarre structures (science fiction etc.) arise from language being dead, "different" themes give illusion of "new" life. Follow roughly outlines in outfanning movement over subject, as river rock, so mindflow over jewel-center need (run your mind over it, *once)* arriving at pivot, where what was dim formed "beginning" becomes sharp-necessitating "ending" and language shortens in race to wire of time-race of work, following laws of Deep Form, to conclusion, last words, last trickle — Night is The End.

MENTAL STATE.   If possible write "without conciousness in semi-trance" (as Yeats' later "trance writing"), allowing subconscious to admit in own uninhibited interesting necessary and so "modern" language what conscious art would censor, and write excitedly, swiftly, with writing-or-typing-cramps, in accordance (as from center to periphery) with laws of orgasm, Reich's "beclouding of consciousness." *Come* from within, out — to relaxed and said.

Belief & Technique for Modern Prose

List of Essentials

1. Scribbled secret notebooks, and wild typewritten pages, for yr own joy
2. Submissive to everything, open, listening
3. Try never get drunk outside yr own house
4. Be in love with yr life
5. Something that you feel will find its own form
6. Be crazy dumbsaint of the mind
7. Blow as deep as your want to blow
8. Write what you want bottomless from bottom of the mind
9. The unspeakable visions of the individual
10. No time for poetry but exactly what is
11. Visionary tics shivering in the chest
12. In tranced fixation dreaming upon object before you
13. Remove literary, grammatical and syntactical inhibition
14. Like Proust be an old teahead of time
15. Telling the true story of the world in interior monolog
16. The jewel center of interest is the eye within the eye
17. Write in recollection and amazement for yourself
18. Work from pithy middle eye out, swimming in language sea
19. Accept loss forever
20. Believe in the holy contour of life
21. Struggle to sketch the flow that already exists intact in mind
22. Dont think of words when you stop but to see picture better
23. Keep track of every day the date emblazoned in yr morning

24. No fear or shame in the dignity of yr experience, language & knowledge
25. Write for the world to read and see yr exact pictures of it
26. Bookmovie is the movie in words, the visual American form
27. In Praise of Character in the Bleak inhuman Loneliness
28. Composing wild, undisciplined, pure, coming in from under, crazier the better
29. You're a Genius all the time
30. Writer-Director of Earthly movies Sponsored & Angeled in Heaven

On Poets & Poetics

The Origins of Joy in Poetry

The new American poetry as typified by the SF Renaissance (which means Ginsberg, me, Rexroth, Ferlinghetti, McClure, Corso, Gary Snyder, Phil Lamantia, Philip Whalen, I guess) is a kind of new-old Zen Lunacy poetry, writing whatever comes into your head as it comes, poetry returned to its origin, in the bardic child, truly ORAL as Ferling said, instead of gray faced Academic quibbling. Poetry & prose had for long time fallen into the false hands of the false. These new pure poets confess forth for the sheer joy of confession. They are CHILDREN. They are also childlike graybeard Homers singing in the street. They SING, they SWING. It is diametrically opposed to the Eliot shot, who so dismally advises his dreary negative rules like the objective correlative, etc. which is just a lot of constipation and ultimately emasculation of the pure masculine urge to freely sing. In spite of the dry rules he set down his poetry itself is sublime. I could say lots more but aint got time or sense. But SF is the poetry of a new Holy Lunacy like that of ancient times (Li Po, Han Shan, Tom O Bedlam, Kit Smart, Blake) yet it also has that mental discipline typified by the haiku (Bashō, Buson), that is, the discipline of pointing out things directly, purely, concretely, no abstractions or explanations, wham wham the true blue song of man.

Introduction to *River of Red Wine* by Jack Micheline

Micheline is a fine new poet, and that's something to crow about. Doctor William Carlos Williams I think would like him, if he heard him read out loud. He has that swinging free style I like, and his tongue gets caught in his mouth and instead of saying 'hill' where you expect 'hill' he says 'mill'. . . what's the use of this odious comparison? I dunno. Ask Doctor Johnson Zen Master Magee of Innisfree. I dunno. Man, this introduction will have to do. I like the poetry of Jack Micheline. See? There is some poetry I don't like, and that's the poetry that's premeditated and crafted and revised and so what you read a lot of . . . you name it. I like the free rhyme, and these sweet lines revive the poetry of open hope in America, by Micheline, tho Whitman and Ginsberg know all that jive, and me too, and there are so many other great poets swinging nowadays (Burroughs, Corso, Steve Tropp I hear, McClure, Duncan, Creeley, Whalen, especially Whalen & Snyder, and Anton Rosenberg, I don't know where to turn and I never pretended to be a critic till now) so I quit and abdicate. Just read what you like anyway. When you sit on a curbstone at dawn on Times Square at age 171, what's the difference, or 17? Right, man? Just look at the sky and say, "As tho I didn't know already."

Statement for *Gasoline* by Gregory Corso

I think that Gregory Corso and Allen Ginsberg are the two best poets in American and that they can't be compared to each other. Gregory was a tough young kid from the Lower East Side who rose like an angel over the rooftops and sang Italian songs as sweet as Caruso and Sinatra but in words. "Sweet Milanese hills" brood in his Renaissance soul, evening is coming on the hills. Amazing and beautiful Gregory Corso, the one & only Gregory the Herald. Read slowly and see.

Statement on Poetics for *The New American Poetry*

Add alluvials to the end of your line when all is exhausted but something has to be said for some specified irrational reason, since reason can never win out, because poetry is NOT a science. The rhythm of how you decide to "rush" yr statement determines the rhythm of the poem, whether it is a poem in verse-separated lines, or an endless one-line poem called prose . . . (with its paragraphs). So let there be no equivocation about statement, and if you think this is not hard to do, try it. You'll find that your lies are heavier than your intentions. And your confessions lighter than Heaven.

Otherwise, who wants to read?

I myself have difficulty covering up my bullshit lies.

Are Writers Made or Born?

Writers are made, for anybody who isn't illiterate can write; but geniuses of the writing art like Melville, Whitman or Thoreau are born. Let's examine the word "genius." It doesn't mean screwiness or eccentricity or excessive "talent." It is derived from the Latin word *gignere* (to beget) and a genius is simply a person who *originates* something never known before. Nobody but Melville could have written *Moby Dick*, not even Whitman or Shakespeare. Nobody but Whitman could have conceived, originated and written *Leaves of Grass;* Whitman was *born* to write a *Leaves of Grass* and Melville was *born* to write a *Moby Dick*. "It ain't whatcha do," Sy Oliver and James Young said, "it's the way atcha' do it." Five thousand writing-class students who study "required reading" can put their hand to the legend of Faustus but only one Marlowe was born to do it the way he did.

I always get a laugh to hear Broadway wiseguys talk about "talent" and "genius." Some perfect virtuoso who can interpret Brahms on the violin is called a "genius," but the genius, the originating force, really belongs to Brahms; the violin virtuoso is simply a talented interpreter — in other words, a "Talent." Or you'll hear people say that so-and-so is a "major writer" because of his "large talent." There can be no major writer without original genius. Artists of genius, like Jackson Pollock, have painted things that have never been seen before. Anybody who's seen his immense Samapattis of color has no right to criticize his "crazy method" of splashing and throwing and dancing around.

Take the case of James Joyce; people said he "wasted" his "talent" on the stream of consciousness style, when in fact he was simply *born* to originate it. How would you like to spend your old age reading books about contemporary life written in the pre-Joycean style of, say, Ruskin, or William Dean Howells, or Taine? Some geniuses come with heavy feet and march solemnly forward like Dreiser, yet no one ever wrote about that America of his as well as he. Geniuses can be scintillating and geniuses can be somber, but it's that inescapable sorrowful depth that shines through — *originality*.

Joyce was insulted all his life by practically all of Ireland and the world for being a genius. Some Celtic Twilight idiots even conceded he had *some* talent. What else could they say, since they were all going to start imitating him? But five thousand university-trained writers could put their hand to a day in June in Dublin in 1904, or one night's dreams, and never do with it what Joyce did with it: he was simply born to do it. On the other hand, if the five thousand "trained" writers, plus Joyce, all put their hands to a *Reader's Digest*-type article about "Vacation Hints" or "Homemaker's Tips," even then I think Joyce would stand out because of his inborn originality of language insight. Bear well in mind what Sinclair Lewis told Thomas Wolfe: "If Thomas Hardy had been given a contract to write stories for the *Saturday Evening Post*, do you think he would have written like Zane Grey or like Thomas Hardy? I can tell you the answer to that one. He would have written like Thomas Hardy. He couldn't have written like anyone else but Thomas Hardy. He would have kept on writing like Thomas Hardy, whether he wrote for *The Saturday Evening Post* or *Captain Billy's Whiz-bang*."

When the question is therefore asked, "Are writers made or born?" one should first ask, "Do you mean writers with talent or writers with originality?" Because anybody can write, but not everybody invents new forms of writing. Gertrude Stein invented a new form of writing and her imitators are just "talents." Hemingway later invented his own form also. The critereon for judging talent or genius is ephemeral, speaking rationally in this world of graphs, but one gets the feeling definitely when a writer of genius amazes him by strokes of force never seen before and yet hauntingly familiar (Wilson's famous "shock of recognition"). I got that feeling from *Swann's Way*, as well as from *Sons and Lovers*. I do not get it from Colette, but I do get it from Dickinson. I get it from Céline, but I do not get it from Camus. I get it from Hemingway, but not from Raymond Chandler, except when he's dead serious. I get it from the Balzac of *Cousine Bette*, but not from Pierre Loti. And so on.

The main thing to remember is that talent imitates genius because there's nothing else to imitate. Since talent can't originate it has to imitate, or interpret. The poetry on page 2 of the *New York Times*, with all its "silent wings of urgency in a dark and seldom wood" and other lapidary trillings, is but a poor imitation of previous poets of genius, like Yeats, Dickinson, Apollinaire, Donne, Suckling. . . .

Genius gives birth, talent delivers. What Rembrandt or Van Gogh saw in the night can never be seen again. No frog can jump in a pond like Bashō's frog. *Born* writers of the future are amazed already at what they're seeing now, what we'll all see in time for the first time, and then see imitated many times by *made* writers.

So in the case of a born writer, genius involves the original formation of a new style. Though the language of Kyd is Elizabethan as far as period goes, the language of Shakespeare can truly be called only *Shakespearean*. Oftentimes an originator of new language forms is called "pretentious" by jealous talents. But it ain't whatcha write, it's the way atcha write it.

Written Address to the Italian Judge

Re: Attorney General vs. Kerouac

I wish to address His Honor in my own manner, that is, in a manner untrained in legal learning and court language. Although I have tried to understand the account of the life-long legal argument between Baron Verulam (Sir Francis Bacon) and Sir Edward Coke, as described in the Eleventh Edition of the Encyclopaedia Britannica, which argument however, I understand, helped to create the basis of English jurisprudence, I could not really make head or tail of the details, not being trained in law study except for occasional idle afternoon library perusals of cases of So-and-So vs. So-and-So involving the collisions of barges et cetera wherein however there is always a perfect settlement based on the available factual evidence.

But I do know this: whatever the decision of the judge may be, "The judge," in the words of Dr. Samuel Johnson addressed to James Boswell, his biographer, "is always right" once the evidence has been weighed and the decision has been made. This is the basis of jurisprudence: "The judge is always right."

I want His Honor to know that I receive no assistance in this written address to the bench.

First, as to the significance of *The Subterraneans*, you have briefs there, cachets, dossiers of aficionados, papers, all shadowed with social overtones, only of controversial value as evidence.

Second, as to the artistic background of *The Subterraneans*: the form is strictly confessional in accordance with the confessional form of Fyodor Dostoevsky's *Notes From the*

Underground. The idea is to tell all about a recently concluded event in all its complexity, at least tell all that can be told
without attempting to offend certain basic sensibilities in
polite society as well as in a society that accedes to, and more
or less votes for, the pacification of instincts such as, say, pacification of the scatological instincts such as, say, the instinct
to open your mouth and show what you're eating (as certain
cretinous people and maniacs do), or the instinct to publicly
describe revolting bodily functions best kept out of sight naturally, or the instinct to deliberately offend the quiet hearts
of others in order to get their attention because of vicious
jealousy sometimes diagnosed as "frustration." In *The
Subterraneans*, when I tell all, I tell within the bounds of insti-
tutionalized, modern, reasonably repentant common sense.
First I pour out confessions of love, how I first met her, what
thoughts and memories were aroused, what I preliminarily
attempted, but never in a language that is anything but
frankly civil as well as civilized, as well as adultly mondaine,
as well as delicately veiled in discussion. There are no
descriptions that tend to ruffle the spine towards further
provocative or salacious hints, no, it's all there purely stated
and then the door is closed to any possible subsequent
description which would offend me, the author, as well as
anyone else concerned in this delicate matter dealing with
delicate matters. I wish to see to it that literature can be complete and yet the door be closed somewhere.

Third, as to the style of *The Subterraneans*: this is the style
I've discovered for narrative art, whereby the author stum-
bles over himself to tell his tale, just as breathlessly as some
raconteur rushing in to tell a whole roomful of listeners what
has just happened, and once he has told his tale he has no
right to go back and delete what the hand hath written, just
as the hand that writes upon the wall cannot go back. This
decision, rather, this vow I made with regard to the practice

of my narrative art frankly, Gentlemen, has its roots in my experience inside the confessionals of a Catholic childhood. It was my belief then that to withhold any reasonably and decently explainable detail from the Father was a sin, although you can be sure that the Father was aware of the difficulties of the delicacy involved. Yet all was well.

I wish the court to review this fact: that the factual evidence in this case is in itself open to interpretation. In the case of a barge ramming a barge, the factual evidence concerns someone at the wheel overlooking a fact of the factor of wind, current, direction, this or that, but none of it is under the shadow of interpretation, because winds, currents, hands in the wheelhouse beg not interpretation.

But in this case, the factual evidence which is the book itself, I beg to remind you, in its entirety and not just in underlined sections for the sake of a prosecutor's brief, is open to interpretation because of the amorphous, chaotic, nay ephemeral nature of narrative art itself. Some like David, some don't, yet David is there (Michelangelo's). Opinions as to the interpretation of the value or non-value of *The Subterraneans* as narrative art, and of *The Subterraneans* as either salacious or non-salacious, are based on opinion merely. I use the word "salacious" instead of the word "obscene" because war, and many other things, are obscene. Obscene is from the Latin *obscaenus*, detestable, unnatural, and from Old English, inauspicious, which can be applied to war, robbery, dishonesty and all sorts of vicious and cruel events, whilst "salacious" is from Latin *salax* or *salacem*, lecherous, and *salire*, to leap, or, leaping lechery. Yet the evidence is there, the book itself. What can a jury do when evidence melts into opinion, and opinion melts into evidence?

In my own opinion, which is mine and mine alone, *The Subterraneans* is an attempt on my part to use spontaneous modern prose to execute the biography of someone else in a given circumstance and time, as completely as possible without offending the humanistic, in any case, human, tastes, of myself or anyone else, for the sake of the entertainment, plus the suffering attention and edification of some reader by the fire of a winter midnight.

In my presentation of the evidence, however, and this is all the evidence there is, I present as exhibit Number One the book itself in its entirety from first sentence to last.

Jack Kerouac, May 23, 1963

Shakespeare and the Outsider

The secret of Shakespeare: two parts: one, he wrote costume poetry for the state — There's your fortune — Had (amongst his Ovids and Montaignes) a copy of Plutarch's Lives and a book about Kings of England, and set the scene like a Hollywood Historical Costume Picture (think what he would have done with DeMille equipments on the Redcoats of Canada, the court of Catherine the Great, Napoleon and the whiff of grapeshot) — Made dandies, couriers, ladies, fools and generals and emperors talk with yapping mouths — a bwa a bwa a bwa BOOM! the cannon offstage. This is poetry, dramatic poetry. The vision of life, in which he was swilled like a pearl in a pigsty, a gloriously magnificent singer. "In peace," he says to the nobles in the boxes, "there's nothing so becomes a man/as modest stillness and humility;/When the blast of war blows in our ears,/then imitate the action of the tiger." — This is like Krishna's advice to the melancholy prince in Bhagavad-Gita. It's given by King Henry V with scaling-ladder in hand, at Walls of Harfleur Act III Sc I, and for reason ". . .you noblest English/Whose blood is fet from fathers of warproof!" — Then our Immortal Bard played the Gallery with Nym — And played a form of *Tao* (Chinese No-Action) with "Boy": —

> BOY: — *Would I were in an alehouse in London! I would give all my fame for a pot of ale and safety.*

Shakespeare's real Gimmick Poetry is in Nym. Boy, Ariel, Clown, Pistol, Fool, the Gravedigger etc. — then, to unfold the story, his monologues and soliloquies unfold the plain explanation concerning the backgrounds of the play. It's just a shining technique in the darkness, and goes out only when the stars go out. Face, if you will, Gentlemen, the stars never mind.

Part two, the singing of "mellifluous and honey tongued Shakespeare": — A teenage boy raped under an Avon apple tree by an older woman, married and then cuckolded via his older brother Edmund Shakespeare the Villain, on the road to London not roomed in the inn, in London holding the reins of the horses outside the theater, is asked "Hey Willie can you come in here and carry a spear?" and later "Will, can you add some lines to that last act?" and finally "Ah Sweet Will, how can you ever top that?"

He stands by himself alone in Heaven as the greatest writer in any language in any country anytime in the history of the world: — "Mankind and this world have never been so sharply sifted or so sternly consoled, since Lucretius, as in Shakespeare's tragedies" (Oliver Elton). — Compared to him Homer groaned, Dante too — Cervantes could not combine drama and poetry in concentrated *spates* individualized like *Othello* or *Hamlet* or *King Henry V* breaking your heart year after year — Tolstoy threw a fit — Goethe marveled and bit his lip — Nietzsche was driven wroth — Dostoevsky sighed — Blake and Smart smiled — The Japanese and Chinese poets would have covered their ears and run wondering from London — Burns quivered — Pound fell into unreasoning jealousy based on Provençal lilts — Donne and Vaughan and Herbert grinned — Chaucer sat up in his grave and glanced curiously that away — Balzac irritably sharpened his pen quill and tried again and marked his master — Villon stared inspired into the future — Molière shrugged and concentrated on mere *mores* — Dickens exulted — Carlyle glared furiously into the dark looking for such light — Masey, Dan Michel and Spenser mourned in their cloaks — Modern idiots like Apollinaire, Mayakovsky and Artaud simply spat at the stars in defiance of him — Johnson nodded — Pope bowed — Melville smiled over the bow — Whitman accepted — Emily Dickinson saying about flowers

Spiciest at fading, indicate
a habit of a laureate

understood, and James Joyce leered to comprehend.

Because (and here I want to present a new theory that really should be looked into by proper technicians of Shakespeare Research), when Shakespeare says "Slaves as ragged as Lazarus in the painted cloth, where the glutton's dog licked his sores," or "Greasy Joan doth keel the pot, and birds sit brooding in the snow" (combining the thought as well as the SOUND of the ellipse of a Japanese *haiku)* or those awful lines conspired around "Tarquin's ravishing strides," or "and pat he comes like the catastrophe of the old comedy," I always wonder "Where did he get that rhythmic sound?" and always think "That's what I like about Shakespeare, where he Raves in the great world night like the wild wind through an old Cathedral" (the *training* of that). Condell and Heminge reported that his handwritten manuscripts were hardly blotted, if at all, as he apparently flowed in his writing and wrote in an inspired hurry what he immediately heard sound-wise while his steeltrap brain kept shutting down on the exigencies of plot and character in that sea of ravening English that came out of him. And my hunch is that in spite of the many ponderous *double entendres* that take some thinking, he did it all more out of intuition, than out of deliberateness and the craftiness of that. My theory is that Joyce fully understood this, the first man to do so since 1615 with the possible exception of Laurence Sterne: — who refused to be austere and severe to cover up the glory of Shakespeare. The prose of Shakespeare, "the most natural and noble of his age," as it appears in the plays, as apart from the verse, did not persist in English literature but languished with its "tendons and sinews of the language" under the avalanche of the "leisurely and amorous romance" of "French influence and example" that became the rage at the time, and was followed by big heavy laborings designed to vigorously counteract so-called Elizabethan "Euphuism," thus alack, the crasser part of English became known as "English prose," on through Johnson, the mathematical canting absurdities that followed, and the prose of the London (and New York) *Times*. Today they find cotton to stuff up one meager idea inside a huge pillow of a paragraph. This dullard's guile is known as "bombast," derived from the Middle French *bombace*, meaning cotton, the stuffing and padding of speech with highsounding words all inflated and fustian and turgid, the long arid clauses grimacing with superiority the useless adverbs deadening satiated verbs ("ineradicably misinformed" or something) the "latters" and "formers" and "a prioris" and "per ses" and "presentlys" and "consequentlys" all told and only for the sake of using cuty-dried phrases a thousand times over without any definite meaning, like in politicians' windbag talk, in a word, CANT. The rich natural hoarse singing, the ringing *complaynt* of the Bard and the very art of it was forgotten for favor of the pursy Drab, and the Pundit, and the very *Grammarian*.

James Joyce over 300 years later attempted to become "Shakespeare in a Dream" and succeeded. *Finnegans Wake* is pure raving Shakespeare below, beneath, all over: — "I no sooner seen a ghist of his frighteousness than I was bibbering with vear a few verset off fooling for fjorg for my fifth foot" — and this which is only the end of a long rant-sentence is pure Shakespeare Sound and Rhythm but with Irish longwinded specialties as dark as the peat in Yeats. "THERES SCARES KNUD IN THIS GNARLD WARLD A FULLY SO SVEND AS DILATES FOR THE IMPROVEMENT OF OUR FOERSES OF NATURE BY YOUR VERY AMPLE SOLVENT OF REFRACTING UPON ME LIKE IS BOESEN FIENND" — Your Webster's Collegiate

Dictionary and even your antique Stormonth Dictionary
won't help you here: — "Pappaist! Gambanman! Take the
cawraidd's blow! Yia! Your partridge's last." — Smash! —
Crash! — Yah! — Cannon offstage, BOOM! — "and"
(Shakespeare) "such as indeed were never soldiers, but dis-
carded unjust serving-men, younger sons to younger brothers, revolted tapsters and ostlers trade-fallen, the cankers of a
calm world and a long peace — " (which passage proves
Shakespeare heard *sound* first then the words were there in
his QUICK HEAD). "Well/ To the latter end of a fray and
the beginning of a feast/ Fits a dull fighter and a keen guest"
he adds — and everybody knows how folk sayings always
seem to pop out of tongue-sounds instead of out of "thinks,"
like in "It's about to clabber up and rain all over" or, "Can't
pour piss out of a boot," or even the old Medieval Quebecois
saying, *"Ya pus plus faim qu'la mer a soif."*

For softer sounds, the divine punner listened to softer
rains in his brain: Duke of Burgundy speaking about France:
— ". . .her fallow leas/ The darnel, hemlock and rank
fumitory/ Doth root upon, while that the coulter rusts/ That
should deracinate such savagery:/ The even mead, that erst
brought sweetly forth/ the freckled cowslip. . ." Or Hamlet
on his father's love of the Queen: ". . .so loving to my
mother/ That he might not beteem the winds of
heaven/ Visit her face too roughly" — (In a sonnet, there
"Since first your eye I eyed") — and in Lear the daughter
mourns like a dove: —

> *. . .to watch — poor*
> *perdu! —*
> *With this thin helm?*

"Every cove to his gentry mort," Shakespeare might have
added, and it was Joyce who wrote that last line, in *Ulysses,*
mindful of how poetry is done by mouthings and brainwaves
and wizardries of inwit and not necessarily always by slow

measured inductive introspections sunk in anguished consultation about shoulds and shouldnots.

But Joyce was never able to combine drama with such poetry, and treacherous plots with sighs like that, and cries, and be, amongst all writers of all time, Divinest Thaumaturgist, Forever.

On Céline

Louis-Ferdinand Céline was a general practitioner in the poor quarters of Paris. He was also highly sensitive and actually a kindly doctor according to my instinct as I read his accounts of the senseless suffering of some of his clientele. The sweet little boy coughing to death . . . the beautiful young girl bleeding to death . . . the old landladies long dead. Reading *Voyage au bout d'la nuit* was to me like seeing the greatest French movie ever made, a super heavenly *Quai des brumes* a thousand times sadder than Jean Gabin's bitter lip or Michel Simon's lugubrious lechery or the carnival where lovers cry . . .

It seemed to me that Céline was actually the most compassionate French writer of his time. He himself said (in 1950) (in a newspaper interview in Paris) that there were only two real writers in France at the time, himself and Jean Genet. He dismissed Genet half-jokingly for the obvious reason known to us all. Yet he was wise enough to recognise Genet. I feel that Genet completed the tragedy of the French Queer Underworld for Balzac, but in Rimbaud's terms, or rather under Rimbaud's terms, and under Villon's critical eye (as Baudelaire watches from a distant balcony). This investigation was something portly Bourgeois master Balzac could never have dared to undertake. And the prose of Genet is every bit as angelic, from the street, as the prose of Proust was angelic from the upper apartment. And I say Céline was right about Genet.

But Céline himself, his sources came from further back in French literature: he came from Rabelais, he even came on through from the virile Hugo. It always seemed to me that Robinson of *Voyage* was being pursued by Shroudy Javert, and that Javert was Céline himself, and Céline himself was Robinson, and therefore *Voyage* is the story of the Shroud of Céline's self pursuing the Shroud of Céline's non-self, Robinson.

I can't see how people could accuse Céline of vitriolic malice if they'd ever read the chapter on the young whore in Detroit, or the agonized priest climbing in through the window in *Mort à crédit*, or that marvelous inventor in the same story.

I say he was a writer of great, supremely great charm and intelligence and no one compares to him. He is the main influence on the writing of Henry Miller, by the way, that modern flamboyant tone of knocking the chip off the shoulder of horror, that sincere agony, that redeeming shrug and laugh. He even made Trotsky laugh and cry. The political crisis of our times is no more important than the Turkish crisis of 1822, when William Blake was writing about the Lamb. In the long run, men will only remember the Lamb. Camus would have had us turn literature into mere propaganda, with his "commitment" talk. I only remember Robinson . . . I only remember the Doctor micturating in the Seine at dawn . . . Myself I'm only an ex-sailor, I have no politics, I dont even vote.

Adieu, pauvre suffrant, mon docteur.

Jack Kerouac

Biographical Notes

For *The New American Poetry*

After my brother died, when I was four, they tell me I began to sit motionlessly in the parlor, pale and thin, and after a few months of sorrow began to play the old Victrola and act out movies to the music. Some of these movies developed into long serial sagas, "continued next week," leading sometimes to the point where I tied myself with rope in the grass and kids coming home from school thought I was crazy. My brother had taught me how to draw so at the age of 8 I began to produce comic strips of my own: "Kuku and Koko at the Earth's Core," (the first, rudely drawn) on to highly developed sagas like "The Eighth Sea." A sick little boy in Nashua N.H. heard of these and wanted to borrow them. I never saw them again. At the age of 11 I wrote whole little novels in nickel notebooks, also magazines (in imitation of *Liberty Magazine)* and kept extensive horse racing newspapers going. The first "serious" writing took place after I read about Jack London at the age of 17. Like Jack, I began to paste up "long words" on my bedroom wall in order to memorize them perfectly. At 18 I read Hemingway and Saroyan and began writing little terse short stories in that general style. Then I read Tom Wolfe and began writing in the rolling style. Then I read Joyce and wrote a whole juvenile novel like *Ulysses* called "Vanity of Duluoz." Then came Dostoevsky. Finally I entered a romantic phase with Rimbaud and Blake which I called my "self-ultimacy" period, burning what I wrote in order to be "Self-ultimate." At the age of 24 I was groomed for the Western idealistic concept of letters from reading Goethe's *Dichtung und Wahrheit*. The discovery of a style of my own based on spontaneous get-with-it, came after reading the marvelous free narrative letters of Neal Cassady, a great writer who happens also to be the Dean Moriarty of *On the Road*. I also learned a lot about unrepressed wordslinging from young Allen Ginsberg and William Seward Burroughs.

For *New American Story*

Parochial schools gave me a good early education that made it possible for me to begin writing stories and even one novel at the age of eleven. These schools, in Lowell, Mass., were called St. Louis de France and St. Joseph. When I got to public schools and college I was already so far advanced I set new records cutting classes in order to go to the library and read all day, or to stay in my room (at college) and write plays. Evidently the progressive education system is wrong, because you only have to learn to read and write, and then you're on your own from the age of 12 or 13 on, from the point of view of 'higher' aims, which can't be taught, only elicited from you by circumstances and influences not necessarily confined to the classroom.

For *Attacks of Taste*

"Which books were your favorites or influenced you most as a teenager and why?"

My earliest childhood reading was Catechism in French, the Bible in French, and *The Little Shepherd of Kingdom Come* . . . plus the Bobbsey Twins and *Rebecca of Sunnybrook Farm* . . . and *Roll River* by James Boyd, and then the later slavering over *The Shadow Magazine*, *Phantom Detective Magazine* and *Street & Smith's Star Western Magazine*.

Observations

"Among the Fantastic Wits . . ."

Among the fantastic wits of the Horace Mann School for Boys in 1939-40 Eddie Gilbert ranked practically number one — I was just an innocent New England athlete boy suddenly thrown into what amounted to an Academy of incunabular Milton Berles hundreds of them wisecracking and ad libbing on all sides. We were all in stitches — The chief claque of official huge wits was led by Dick Sheresky, Burt Stollmack, and Morty Maxwell, but when mention of Eddie Gilbert was made there fell a kind of stricken convulsion just at the thought of him — he was insanely witty — So much so that now, today, as I read about his recent escapade with the two million dollars I laugh, not because I think it's funny but because *Eddie* is so funny, it seems almost as though he'd pulled this last fantastic joke to tear the funnyguys of Horace Mann apart for once and for all (in some dim way at the back of his mind when he absconded to Brazil I believe this to be true).

Prep school humor is always a little insular: at Horace Mann that year we found it in using and toasting the names of classmates who were not "wits" and were not "athletes" but were obscure behind their spectacles studying butterflies in the library or discussing the history of the Thuringian Flagellants with Professor Thus And Such at dusk, whose names, although often hilarious in themselves, were infinitely more hilarious when you thought of their activities about the campus.

In the 1940 Horace Mann Yearbook "The Horace Mannikin" Eddie is described as a "speedy, clever" varsity soccer player at the inside position — You see a picture of him with wild curly hair grinning with the soccer team — He is also described as the number two varsity tennis player but I think he was actually number one later in the season — At his father's estate later on near Manhasset he had a famous pro come to give him lessons during a class reunion on his long lawn that fell away to Long Island Sound. And Eddie was a smooth player. — In the Yearbook there's also a picture of him playing the violin and a mention of the fact that he was the best jazz dancer, or "shagger," in the class at the time. — The "SENIOR OPINIONS" in the Yearbook list as follows: "BEST DANCER, Ed Gilbert . . . DONE H.M. FOR MOST, Ed Gilbert . . . HARDEST SHIRKER, Ed Gilbert . . . THINKS HE'S MOST SOPHISTICATED, Ed Gilbert". . . signs of his very great intrinsic popularity considering the other categories for nomination such as MOST RESPECTED, LEAST APPRECIATED.

In 1940 he took me on weekends to his parents' house then in Flushing and I happened to mention to his handsome quiet father that I had never seen a hundred dollar bill and he, a successful dealer in lumber, removed a 100 dollar bill from his wallet and let me examine it — I wrote English term papers for Eddie at $2 a throw, also for several others.

Eddie threw a big Class reunion in 1947 at his estate near Manhasset — About thirty of us drank, swam, played a game of softball, and then at the toasting time at the long table funny Eddie stood up and proposed a toast to "Phil Greilsamer, Rudy Henning, Harry Allison, Ivy King, etcetera" and, turning to me, "Jackie Kerouac."

I said "How about Rudo Globus, Bob Bartz, Male Bersohn, Marty Beller, Dick Blum, Shel Blumenkrantz, Dave Haft, etcetera and that old Jesuit underdog Patrick Edlow McCue?" — and for the last time we were all rolling under the table in stitches — because after that, the young businessmen went their separate ways and now we are all middleaged in one pickle or another.

When boys are 17 or 16 years old, how blue their eyes! what mists! what believing mists lie there like Land O Lakes poems! pimples or not on the chin you're drawn to those believing sweet futury hope eyes!

The limousines of the Nazarenes! the foulard ties! the London wools!

The sad thing is, though I could weep tears to think of my boyhood New England summernight trees swishing at my starry window of clear eyed pure hope, I could almost weep as many tears to think of Eddie's room in the old home in Flushing (jokes he made about Flushing, even): the neat little boy-bedroom curtains, the swell dresser full of clean socks and shirts the brass handles clicking significantly and softly rich, the closet full of tennis sneakers and rich golden shoe trees making me grip my breast, and the tennis racket on the wall — The smell of bacon and eggs downstairs when we woke up on Saturday mornings — the fresh rain on the front lawn — Eddie bouncing around joking with the maid — the screened porch — For all his kidding around a kind of pale green clarity in the sincerity of his gaze — Nobody'll ever know America completely because nobody ever knew Gatsby, I guess.

Moonlight on the lawn, J. D. Salinger middleclass livingrooms with the lights out, futile teenage doubledate smooching in the dark, poor Eddie and I appeared at that queer era in 20th Century America just before the girls started to chase the boys down the street — It was the time when you would boast about how long you "necked" last night — Enough to drive anybody to "theft" or "suicide" in later years or any kind of subliminal "theft" or "suicide" or suicide pure and simple . . .

Another strange circumstance: Eddie and I were on the

Horace Mann chess team and sat and demolished the Fieldston team one strange red winter late afternoon in the Fieldston library not daring to look up at each other from our enemy boards lest we start rolling on the floor and lose our queens . . .

When Wall Street's Walter Gutman told me about two years ago that Eddie had become a "financial wizard" I wasn't surprised — We'd both decided to become wizards at something or other as we giggled in the halls of Horace Mann among all the other wizards of that class: from dopey funny kids they've all grown to horrendous stature as formidable restauranteurs, realtors, department store tycoons, some scientists, future Balzacs, future furnitures . . .

But Eddie's style in the halls of the school is what I think of: Eddie used to come breezing and bouncing down the hall by himself with a wicked little pale grin and rush by as everybody yelled at him to stop: he was too busy: in other words he was so funny the academies of Wits waited for him in the hall: even the football players (no slouches at being crazy themselves) also watched him with grins; he was always rushing and serious faced.

He rushed down the hall all the way.

Not Long Ago Joy Abounded at Christmas

I think the celebration of Christmas has changed within the short span of my own lifetime. Only 20 years ago, before World War II, it seems to me Christmas was still being celebrated with a naive and joyous innocence whereas today you hear the expression, "Christmas comes once a year like taxes." Christmas was observed all-out in my Catholic French-Canadian environment in the 1930s much as it is today in Mexico. At first I was too young to go to midnight mass, but that was the real big event we hoped to grow up to. Until then we'd stay in our beds pretending to be asleep till we heard the parents leaving for midnight mass then we'd come down and sneak a look at our toys, touching them and putting them back in place, and rush up again in the dark in gleeful pajamas tittering when we heard them come back again, usually now with a big gang of friends for the open house party.

When we were old enough it was thrilling to be allowed to stay up late on Christmas Eve and put on best suits and dresses and overshoes and earmuffs and walk with the adults through crunching dried snow to the bell-ringing church. Parties of people laughing down the street, bright throbbing stars of New England winter bending over rooftops sometimes causing long rows of icicles to shimmer as we passed. Near the church you could hear the opening choruses of Bach being sung by child choirs mingled with the grownup choirs usually led by a tenor who inspired laughter more than anything else. But from the wide-open door of the church poured golden light and inside the little girls were lined up for their trumpet choruses caroling Handel.

My favorite object in the church was the statue of the saint holding little Jesus in his arms. This was the statue of St. Antoine de Padue but I always thought it was St. Joseph and felt that it was quite just that he should get a chance to hold Him in his arms. My eyes always strayed to his statue, he who now with demure plaster countenance, holding the insubstantial child with face too small and body too doll like, pressed cheek against the painted curls, supporting in mid-air lightly against his mysterious infinite breast the Son, downward looking into candles, agony, the foot of the world where we knelt in dark vestments of winter, all the angels and calendars and spirey altars behind him, his eyes lowered to a mystery he himself wasn't let in on, yet he'd go along in the belief that poor St. Joseph was clay to the Hand of God (as I thought), a humble self-admitting truthful saint — with none of the vain freneticisms of the martyrs, a saint without glory, guilt, accomplishment or Franciscan charm — a self-effacing grave and demure ghost in the Arcades of Christendom — he who knew the desert stars, and spat with the Wise Men in back of the barn — arranger of the manger, old hobo saint of haylofts and camel trails — my secret Friend. Now in midnight mass I gloried proudly in his new honorable position at the front of the church, standing over his family in the manger where all eyes were turned.

After mass the open house was on. Gangs would troop back home or to other houses. Collectors for a Christmas organization of Medieval origin and preserved by the French of Quebec and New England called "La Guignolee," and now sponsored by the Society for the Poor, St. Vincent de Paul, would appear at these open house parties and collect old clothes and food for the poor and never turn down a glass of sweet red wine with a crossignolle (cruller) and even join in singing in the kitchen. They always sang an old canticle of their own before leaving. The Christmas trees were always huge in those days, the presents were all laid out and opened at a given consensus. What glee I'd feel to see the clean white shirts of my adults, their flushed faces, the laughter, the bawdy joking around. Meanwhile the avid women were in the kitchen with aprons over best dresses getting out the tortierres (pork pies) from the icebox. Days of preparation had gone into these sumptuous and delicious pies, which are better cold than hot. Also my mother would make immense ragouts de boulettes (pork meatball stew with carrots and potatoes) and serve that piping hot to crowds of sometimes 12 or 15 friends and relatives: her aluminum drip grind coffee pot made 15 large cups. Also from the icebox came bowls of freshly made freshly cooled cortons (French-Canadian for paté de maison), a spread to go on good fresh crusty bread liberally baked around town at several French bakeries.

In the general uproar of gifts and unwinding of wrappers it was always a delight to me to step out on the porch or even go up the street a ways at 1:00 in the morning and listen to the silent hum of heaven diamond stars, watch the red and green windows of homes, consider the trees that seemed frozen in sudden devotion, and think over the events of another year passed. Before my mind's eye was the St. Joseph of my imagination clasping the darling little Child.

Perhaps too many battles have been fought on Christmas Eve since then — or maybe I'm wrong and little children of 1957 secretly dig Christmas in their little devotional hearts.

Home at Christmas

It's a Sunday afternoon in New England just three days before Christmas — Ma's making the roast in the kitchen range, also tapioca pudding so when Sister Nin comes in from outdoors with the shovel she's been wielding in the blizzard there are cold waves of snowy air mixing with the heat steams of tapioca over the stove and in my mouth I can taste whipped cream cold from the icebox on the hot pudding tonight.

While Ma cooks she also sits at the round kitchen table reading the *Boston American* — Pa's in the parlor playing the Gospel Singers of Sunday cigarsmoke funnies time — I'm getting ready to take my big blizzard walk into the Massachusetts Shroud begins just down the end of dirt road Phebe Avenue, I'm rummaging in the closet for my hockey stick which will be my walking-stick and feeling-stick to find where puddles and creeklets have disappeared under two feet of snow this day.

"Where you goin'?"

"Take my walk."

"Be careful don't fall in the ice — You're goin' to your Pine Brook? — Oh you're crazy you!" (exasperation)

I start out, down the porch steps, overshoes, woolcap, coat, corduroy pants, mittens — There are Christmas wreaths in all the windows of sweet Phebe — No sign of G.J. or Billy with the kids sliding on the park slope, no sign of them on their porch except G.J.'s sister in her coat all wrapped communing with the plicking fall of vast snows in a silence of her own, girl-like, watching it pile on the porch rail, the little rills, sadnesses, mysteries — She waves — I plod down off our Sis-shoveled walk into Mrs. Quinn's unshoveled walk

where the going is deep, profound, happy — No shoveled
walks all the way to Billy's where bigbrother sixfoot Jack
has worked in muffler with pink cheeks and white teeth,
laughing — Black birds in the black cherry tree, and in the
new snow breadcrumbs, bird tweak tracks, a little dot of kitty
yellow, a star blob of plopsnow ball against Old MacArthur's
wreathy front door — O the clean porches of New England
in the holy dry snow that's drifting across new painted planks
to pile in corners over rubber doormats, sleds, overshoes —
The steam in the windows, the frost, the faces looking out
— And over the sandbank now and down on semi-snow-
plowed Phebe comes the great fwoosh of hard stormwind
from the river cracking leafless shrubs in stick-unison, throwing swirls of coldsifted power, pure, the freezing freshness
everywhere, the sand frozen solid underneath —

Down at the end of Phebe I'm in the middle of the road
now preparing my big Arab strides for the real business of
crossing miles of field and forest to my wanted Brook which
in summer's a rendezvous of swimmers crossing gold and
greenleaf day, bees of bugs, hay, haze, but now the gigantic
Snow King has laid his drape upon the world, locked it in
new silence, all you hear is the profound higher-than-human-
ear screaming of snow radios bedazzling and electrifying the
air like orgones and spermatazoas in a Universe Dance —
They start black specks from heaven, swirl to avoid my gaze,
fall white and ploppy on my nose — I turn my face up to the
sweet soft kiss of Heaven — My feet are getting cold. I hurry
on — Always with a smile of my numb cheeks and pinked
lips I think (remembering movies) how really comfortable it
would be to lie down and go to sleep in the soft thick snow,
head rested — I plod, the hockey stick trails after — I go
through the sandbank draw and rise to survey the sand field
bordered on the other side by a cut of earth with saplings and
boulders — I cluck up my horse and off we gallop in a snow-

bound Westerner to the scene, deep, the sand field is all milky creamy waves of smooth level snow, my blasphemous impertinence tracks make a sad plod in the smoothness — I jump up the cut, stand to survey further vast fields stretching a mile to the wall of pines, the forest of Pine Brook in the unbelievable riot murk beyond, the momentous swing of other swirlstorms.

One last look at Phebe, turning, I see the sweet rooftops of life, of man, of mother and father and children, my heart aches to go back home, I see the dear smokewhip of chimneys, the innocent fall of snow from roofs, the bedangled icicles, the little piteous fences outlined in all that numb null white, the tracks of people, the gleeful steplets of humans twinkling and twittering across the snow and already again over the sandbank ridge a great pall of wind and snow sweeping to fill holes with soft new outline — The mystery — Tears in my eyes from cold and wonder I turn and strike across the plain — The grief of birch that's bent and wintering, the strange mist — Far off the white story frame house in the pine woods stands proud, families are in there furying, living —

The left field of our baseball field is lost — Where the spring bubbles from short right I can see just snow and just one hint of blackening snow where waters below have formed a slush and darking ice — Behind me now I can see my footsteps in silence and sadness of white distance filling, forming, growing vaguer, returning to the macrocosmos of even snow from the microcosmos of my striving — and far back of that and now by distance seeable where before by nearness not, the vague unbelievable hardly-discernible caped gray smoke stacks of the mills across the river and the dim smoke urging to rise from their warm Dickensian interiors of grime, labor, personal involvements among dye vats to the universe of the blizzard oversweeping all —

I reach the end of the plain, go up the wagon path past the backstop homeplate pines, the rocks, past the Greek farm on the left now stilled from Cretan ripple olive peace of summers to frost squat Winter — The top of the hill, the view of the woods, the descent into the woods — The pond at the bottom of the hill, the star beneath the ice in the bottom of the pond, the ice skaters thronging by, an old La Salle with a mattress in the back clonking by and sloshing in the snowplow's flat — I circle the pond, the houses, the French Canadian *paisans* are stomping their feet on still-screened porches, Christmas trees on their backs — Merry Christmas zings in the air — It darkens, dusk's about to come, I've got to hurry, the first heartbreaking Christmas light comes on red and blue in a little farm window across the locked pond — My nose snuffles, my hands the back of em are like thronged red leather — Off the road and into the country path, the fear of shrouded woods ahead — No more houses now, just bushes and pines and boulders and occasional clearings, occasional woodpiles beautifully wreathed with a snow crown — The jump over the little property wire fence, the old tree base where black rocks of Indian Summer kid fires show stark dark through iced snowtops, remnant pieces of charred wood, the pine fronds gray as dead birds — Somewhere above, the coalblack crow is yawking, cr-a-a-a-ck, c-r-a-a-ck, I see the flop of raven twit limbs battering onward through treetop twigs of aerial white to a hole in the heart of the forest, to the central pine and pain of my aching desire, the real Christmas is hiding somewhere from me and it it still, it is holy, it is dark, it is insane, the crow broods there, some Nativity darker than Christianity, with Wise Men from underground, a Virgin Mary of the ice and snow, a Joseph of the trees, a Jesus like a star — a Bethlehem of pinecones, rocks, snakes — Stonewalls, eyes —

But dark gray is the nightfall reality now, I plow my hockey stick in front of me, sometimes it sinks three feet in culverts, holes — I jump and stagger and grind — Now a solid wall of pine is overhead, through the dark skinny limbs I can see loured gloomy night is overshadowing the blizzard's white shadow — Darker, deeper, the forest densens like a room — Numbbuzzing silences ring my ears, I pause to listen, I hear stars — I hear one dog, one farmerdoor slam a mile away — I hear a hoot of sledders, a keen shrill of littlegirl — I hear the tick of snowflake on snow, on limb — Ice is forming on my eyebrows — I come haunting, emerging from the forest, go down the hill to the brook, the stonewall has crystal icing in the heavy winter dim — Black bleak lines in the sky — my mouth is awed open, vapors puff out, it's stopped snowing and I've begun to sense a blue scene in the new night — Soon I see one star above — I reach the brook, it flows under jagged ice caps black as ink, gurgly, silver at the ice rim, cold steaming between blanketwhite banks to its destinations and rivers down — I follow in the gloom — Our diving board's all white, alone, unsupple, stiffwooded in wintertime — Our trapeze hangs looping, dull, iceroped —

"Aaooo!" I yell in the one-room world — My stick penetrates no bottom, I've found a traphole, I walk around cautiously, follow the river bank — Suddenly there's an orange feeling in the air, the sun somewhere has pirouetted protruding limbs into the mass of brass and iron blizzards, silver's being rouged by the blast-works of the real hidden tropic sky — An Arabian Nights blue spreads blue-icing in the West, the Eve-star sparks and shivers in the blanket, one lank icicle suddenly stabs from its center to the earth, dissolves. Cold. No more snowfalls, now the faint howl winds of the New England bring Alaskan shivers from the other hill, down my collar.

I leave the black brook, see the first and last touch of orange on the deepwaters, I know it's beautiful now and everything is good, I hurry back to my city — The path follows the brook, turns off in tangled tragic brushwood, goes deep across a cornfield — I hurry in a semi circling road back across my pond jumping path to the top of Moody Street where again the snowplow's work is piled in double rumps each side, my liberated feet moving in snowshoe flopping jingling gladness — There stands the white Colonial house, on the iron lawn the Christmas-glittering spruce, the noble snowy porch, fresh beginnings of a cocktail party inside — I've reached the top of the hill overlooking all Lowell.

And there she is in the keen blue winter-night, be-starred above, the round brown sadface of the City Hall clock in her granite tower a mile and a half away, the speechless throat of throbbing red neons against distant redbrick of bowling alleys, business, Squares, Chinese restaurants — the giant river scything white and black around, from wilderness of hoar to wilderness of hoar and sea — The thunder and the rumble everywhere in the roundandround horizon phantom night, the distant snake of a hundred-car freight (Boston & Maine), the clean snow smoke in the new snow plain, the red glow of the locomotive's boilers, the distant two-long-one-short-one-long howl at a countryroad crossing, the lone wee caboose at the rear drawn to other worlds, to deeper night — The blue mill eternity windows, sighing froth of falls, reflections of the city actual sad in river's ice — And the one long thoroughfare Moody Street from my feet ribboning clear down Pawtucketville suburb and over the river and down the dense fantastic humaned Little Canada to the downtown thrill — Clear. Cold. Immortal.

I start home down the middle of the plowed street, joyous cries on all sides of sliding kids, the run, the thap of feet, the slap of the sled down, the crumpy ride of the runners over nostalgic snow, rock scrapes, sparks like stars — The scarved bundled gleechildren of New England screeching, the black and white fantasy of their turmoil — Sister Marie is yelling irritably at her brother Ray down the level ice wood of the tenement "Yes, I'm going, yes I'm going, I told you a hundred times!" The wash hangs stiff and frozen, long underwear stands by itself hanged, brown porchlights are on where the mother is packing the frozen wash in fragrant piles — Little tiny nameless infant bundled-to-the ears sits brooding in the snow like Shakespeare's bird, the wreathed window's golden with Christmas behind him, he's looking and wondering: "Where was I born and what is my name? Roland Lambert? Roland Lambert? Who is that, Roland Lambert? Who are you Roland? Hello Mister that passes — " I wave my hand, my footsteps squeak and squidge in the tight-packed snow — I come down deeper in the joy of people.

Past Mr. Vernon, the white houses, the spruce, the lost parochial white yard of night, the concrete wall, the first grocery store — Screams, snow slush, traffic ahead of me — Oilstove heat rushes down dim hallways, out the raw door — There's Al Roberts throwing a snowball at Joe Plouffe, another one, crazy crisscrossing snowballs, hoots, whoopees — The boys are ducking into the brown scarred door of the club for a brew — There's Jim with his Christmas tree, his rubbers are too low, the snow spills into his shoes, against his silk socks, he yells: "Last damn time I'm gonna buy a Christmas tree!" Mrs.T. is yelling to Mrs.H. across the wash rope of the court: "What time ya goin?" — Doors slam, buses ball by, cars race motors in drifts sending blue exhaust in the blue purity — Keen. That same star shudders exploding on the roof of the church where candles flicker — There go the old ladies of the parish to their evening vespers, bundled in black coats, white faced, gray brushed-back hair, their poor little fragile hands hidden in muffs of indoor prayer — Golden light spills from Blezan's store onto the scuffled sidewalk where the gang stands wrangling. I go in to buy my

Old Nick and Clark's, browse at my usual comic books and pulp magazines — The wood stove is red hot in the back, there's the smell of heated overshoes, snow wet floors, infolded night, smoke — I hurry down Gershom, past the snowball fights, the yoohoos, the proud adults in big coats bundling off to social evenings, adjusting scarves, opening garage doors, guffawing — The rosy faced girls are hurrying to the bus, the show, the dance — Sad is the long fence of the long yard and the great high white frozen tree where the sick boy lives — I see him in the window, watching — Little narrow Sarah Avenue hasn't got a window that's not red or green or blue, not one sidewalk unmusical with shovels — Wearily I come to the corner, turn up Phebe, my three mile circle's complete, come to my house on slow wet sodden feet, glad —

Everything is saved. There's heat and warm joy in my house. I linger at the window looking in. My heart breaks to see they're moving so slowly, with such dear innocence within, they don't realize time and death will catch them — not now. Ma moves to lift the pot with such a bemused and serious hardly-knowing goodness and sadness — My father's huge still presence, his thighs in the chair, the absent-minded dark-in-thought face, so wordless, unexplainable, sad — My sister bending over her adolescent fingernails so preoccupied, ravenously attentive in the dream — When I open the door they look up blandly, with blue eyes — I stand facing them all red-faced and frozen —

"Well, it's about time! You missed your supper! — The roast is in the oven, it's not as hot any more — Your mashed potatoes are almost cold — Sit down, crazy!"

I sit at the sparkling table in the bright warm light, ready. She brings me a big helping, glass of milk, bread, butter, tapioca pudding with whipped cream.

"When you're finished eating we're going to go get the Christmas tree and put it up, ah?"

"Yes!"

"Eat, honey, after your big walk you must be hungry."

That night in bed I can still see the great bulging star white as ice beating in the dark field of heaven among the lesser glittering arrays. I can see its reflection in an icicle that depends from an eave above my window, I can hear my winter apple tree cracking black limbs in frost, see the Milky Way all far and cold and cragdeep in Time — I smell the softcoal heat of the furnace in the cellar — Soon dawn, the rosy spread over pure snowfields, the witless winter bird with his muffly feathers inward — My sleep is deep in New England wintertime night.

The Beginning of Bop

Bop began with jazz but one afternoon somewhere on a side-walk maybe 1939, 1940, Dizzy Gillespie or Charley Parker or Thelonious Monk was walking down past a men's clothing store on 42nd Street or South Main in L.A. and from the loudspeaker they suddenly heard a wild impossible mistake in jazz that could only have been heard inside their own imaginary head, and that is a new art. Bop. The name derives from an accident, America was named after an Italian explorer and not after an Indian king. Lionel Hampton had made a record called "Hey Baba Ree Bop" and everybody yelled it and it was when Lionel would jump in the audience and whale his saxophone at everybody with sweat, claps, jumping fools in the aisles, the drummer booming and belaboring on his stage as the whole theater rocked. Sung by Helen Humes it was a popular record and sold many copies in 1945, 1946. First everyone looked around then it happened — bop happened — the bird flew in — minds went in — on the streets thousands of new-type hepcats in red shirts and some goatees and strange queerlooking cowboys from the West with boots and belts, and the girls began to disappear from the street — you no longer saw as in the Thirties the wrangler walking with his doll in the honkytonk, now he was alone, rebop, bop, came into being because the broads were leaving the guys and going off to be middleclass models. Dizzy or Charley or Thelonious was walking down the street, heard a noise, a sound, half Lester Young, half raw-rainy-fog that has that chest-shivering excitement of shack, track, empty lot, the sudden vast Tiger head on the woodfence rainy no-school Saturday morning dumpyards, "Hey!" and rushed off dancing.

On the piano that night Thelonious introduced a wooden

off-key note to everybody's warmup notes, Minton's Playhouse, evening starts, jam hours later, 10 P.M., colored bar and hotel next door, one or two white visitors some from Columbia some from Nowhere — some from ships — some from Army Navy Air Force Marines — some from Europe — The strange note makes the trumpeter of the band lift an eyebrow. Dizzy is surprised for the first time that day. He puts the trumpet to lips and blows a wet blur —

"Hee ha ha!" laughs Charley Parker bending down to slap his ankle. He puts his alto to his mouth and says "Didn't I tell you?" — with jazz of notes . . . Talking eloquent like great poets of foreign languages singing in foreign countries with lyres, by seas, and no one understands because the language isn't alive in the land yet — Bop is the language from America's inevitable Africa, *going* is sounded like *gong*, Africa is the name of the flue and kick beat, off to one side — the sudden squeak uninhibited that screams muffled at any moment from Dizzy Gillespie's trumpet — do anything you want — drawing the tune aside along another improvisation bridge with a reach-out tear of claws, why be subtle and false?

The band of 10 PM Minton's swings into action, Bird Parker who is only 18 year old has a crew cut of Africa looks impossible has perfect eyes and composures of a king when suddenly you stop and look at him in the subway and you can't believe that bop is here to stay — that it is real, Negroes in America are just like us, we must look at them understanding the exact racial counterpart of what the man is — and figure it with histories and lost kings of immemorial tribes in jungle and Fellaheen town and otherwise and the sad mutts sleeping on old porches in Big Easonburg woods where just 90 years ago old Roost came running calling "Maw" through the fence he'd just deserted the Confederate Army and was running home for pone — and flies on watermelon porches. And educated judges in hornrimmed glasses reading the

Amsterdam News.

The band realized the goof of life that had made them be not only mis-placed in a white nation but mis-noticed for what they really were and the goof they felt stirring and springing in their bellies, suddenly Dizzy spats his lips tight-drum together and drives a high screeching fantastic clear note that has everybody in the joint look up — Bird, lips hanging dully to hear, is turning slowly in a circle waiting for Diz to swim through the wave of the tune in a toneless complicated wave of his own grim like factories and atonal at any minute and the logic of the mad, the sock in his belly is sweet, the rock, zonga, monga, bang — In white creamed afternoons of blue Bird had leaned back dreamily in eternity as Dizzy outlined to him the importance of becoming Mohammedans in order to give a solid basis of *race* to their ceremony, "Make that rug swing, mother, — When you say Race bow your head and close your eyes." Give them a religion no Uncle Tom Baptist — make them wearers of skull caps of respectable minarets in actual New York — picking hashi dates from their teeth — Give them new names with zonga sounds — make it weird —

Thelonious was so weird he wandered the twilight streets of Harlem in winter with no hat on his hair, sweating, blowing fog — In his head he heard it all ringing. Often he heard whole choruses by Lester. There was a strange English kid hanging around Minton's who stumbled along the sidewalk hearing Lester in his head too — hours of hundreds of developing choruses in regular beat all day so in the subway no dissonance could crash against unalterable choruses in implacable bars — erected in mind's foundation jazz.

The tune they were playing was *All the Things You Are* . . . they slowed it down and dragged behind it at half tempo dinosaur proportions — changed the placing of the note in the middle of the harmony to an outer more precarious posi-

tion where also its sense of not belonging was enhanced by
the general atonality produced with everyone exteriorizing
the tune's harmony, the clonk of the millennial piano like
anvils in Petrograd — "Blow!" said Diz, and Charley Parker
came in for his solo with a squeaky innocent cry. Monk
punched anguished nub fingers crawling at the keyboard to
tear up foundations and guts of jazz from the big masterbox,
to make Charley Parker hear his cry and sigh — to jar the
orchestra into vibrations — to elicit gloom from the doom of
the black piano. He stared down wild eyed at his keys like a
matador at the bull's head. Groan. Drunken figures shaded in
the weaving background, tottering — the boys didn't care.
On cold corners they stood three backs to one another, facing
all the winds, bent — lips don't care — miserable cold and
broke — waiting like witchdoctors — saying, "Everything
belongs to me because I am poor." Like 12 Century monks
high in winter belfries of the Gothic Organ they wildeyed
were listening to their own wild sound which was heralding
in a new age of music that would eventually require sym-
phonies, schools, centuries of technique, declines and falls of
master-ripe styles — the Dixieland of Louis Armstrong sixteen in New Orleans and of big Pops Forest niggerlips jim in
the white shirt whaling at a big scarred bass in raunchy non-
gry New Orleans on South Rampart street famous for
parades and old Perdido Street — all that was mud in the
river Mississippi, pasts of 1910 gold rings, derby hats of workers, horses steaming turds near breweries and saloons,
— Soon enough it would leap and fill the gay Twenties like
champagne in a glass, pop! — And crawl up to the Thirties
with tired Rudy Vallees lamenting what Louis had laughed in
a Twenties Transoceanic Jazz, sick and tired early Ethel
Mermans, and old beat bedsprings creaking in that stormy
weather blues when people lay in bed all day and moaned
and had it good — The world of the United States was tired

of being poor and low and gloomy in a line. Swing erupted as the Depression began to crack, it was the year marijuana was made illegal, 1937. Young teenagers took to the first restraint, the second, the third, some still wandered on hobo trains (lost boys of the Thirties numbered in the hundreds of thousands. Salvation Armies put up full houses every night and some were ten years old) — teenagers, alienated from their parents who have suddenly returned to work and for good to get rid of that dam old mud of the river — and tear the rose vine off the porch — and paint the porch white — and cut the trees down — castrate the hedges — burn the leaves — build a wire fence — get up an antenna — listen — the alienated teenager in the 20th Century finally ripe gone wild modern to be rich and prosperous no more just around the corner — became the hepcat, the jitterbug, and smoked the new law weed. World War II gave everybody two pats of butter in the morning on a service tray, including your sister. Up from tired degrading swing wondering what happened between 1937 and 1945 and because the Army'd worked it canned it played it to the boys in North Africa and raged it in Picadilly bars and the Andrew sisters put the corn on the can — swing with its heroes died — and Charley Parker, Dizzy Gillespie and Thelonious Monk who were hustled through the chow lines — came back remembering old goofs — and tried it again — and Zop! Dizzy screamed, Charley squealed, Monk crashed, the drummer kicked, dropped a bomb — the bass questionmark plunked — and off they whaled on Salt Peanuts jumping like mad monkeys in the gray new air. "Hey Porkpie, Porkpie, Hey Porkpie!"

"Skidilibee-la-bee you, — oo, — e bop she bam, ske too ria — Parasakiliaoolza — menooriastibatiolyait — oon ya koo." They came into their own, they jumped, they had jazz and took it in their hands and saw its history vicissitudes and developments and turned it to their weighty use and heavily carried it clanking like posts across the enormity of a new world philosophy and a new strange and crazy grace came over them, fell from the air free, they saw pity in the hole of heaven, hell in their hearts, Billy Holliday had rocks in her heart, Lester droopy porkpied hung his horn and blew bop lazy ideas inside jazz had everybody dreaming (Miles Davis leaning against the piano fingering his trumpet with a cigarette hand working making raw iron sound like wood speaking in long sentences like Marcel Proust) — "Hey Jim," and the stud comes swinging down the street and says he's real *bent* and he's *down* and he has a *twisted* face, he works, he wails, he bops, he bangs, this man who was sent, stoned and stabbed is now *down, bent* and *stretched-out* — he is home at last, his music is here to stay, his history has washed over us, his imperialistic kingdoms are coming.

Nosferatu (Dracula)

Nosferatu is an evil name suggesting the red letters of hell
— the sinister pieces of it like "fer" and "eratu" and "nos"
have a red and heinous quality like the picture itself (which
throbs with gloom), a masterpiece of nightmare horror photographed fantastically well in the old grainy tones of brown-
and-black-and-white.

It's not so much that the woods are "misty" but that they
are bright shining Bavarian woods in the morning as the
young jerk hero hurries in a Transylvanian coach to the castle
of the Count. Though the woods be bright you feel evil lurking behind every tree. You just know the inner sides of dead
trees among the shining living pines have bats hanging
upsidedown in torpid sated sleep. There's a castle right
ahead. The hero has just had a drink in a Transylvanian tav-
ern and it would be my opinion to suggest "Don't drink too
deep in Transylvanian taverns!" The maids in the inn are as
completely innocent as Nosferatu is completely evil. The
horses drawing the coach cavort, the youth stretches in the
daytime woods, glad . . . but! . . . *the little traveled road!* The
castle coach transfers him at Charlie Chaplin speed to the
hungry cardinal of vampires. The horses are hooded! They
know that vampire bats will clamp against their withers by
nightfall! They rush hysterically through a milky dimming
forest of mountain dusk, you suddenly see the castle with
bats like flies round the parapet. The kid rushes out looking
for to go find his gory loss. In a strange wool cap a thin
hawknosed man opens the big oaken door. He announces his
servants are all gone. The audience realizes this is Count
Nosferatu himself! Ugh! The castle has tile floors: — somehow there's more evil in those tile floors than in the dripping

dust of later Bela Lugosi castle where women with spiders on their shoulders dragged dead muslin gowns across the stone. They are the tile floors of a Byzantine Alexandrian Transylvanian throat-ogre.

The Count Nosferatu has the long hook nose of a Javelin vampire bat, the large eyes of the Rhinolophidae vampire bat, long horsey mouth looking like it's full of W-shaped cusps with muggly pectinated teeth and molars and incisors like Desmondontae vampire bats with a front tooth missing the better to suck the blood, maybe with the long brush-tipped tongue of the *sanguisuga* so sanguine. He looks in his hunched swift walk like he probably also has his intestinal tract specially modified in accordance with his nocturnal habits . . . the general horrid hare-lipped look of the Noctilio . . . small guillotines in his mouth . . . the exceeding thinness of his gullet. His hands are like the enormous claws of the Leporinus bat and keep growing longer and longer finger-nails throughout the picture.

Meanwhile the kid rushes around enjoying the scenery: — little dusty paths of the castle by day, but by twilight?

The Count plunges to sign his deeds with that thirsty eagerness of the Vampire.

The kid escapes over the wall just in time . . .

The scene shifts to Doktor Van Hellsing in sunny class-room Germany nevertheless photographed as dark as Wolf-bane or the claws that eat a fly. Then it goes to a gorgeously filmed dune where women's Victorian dresses flutter in the fresh sea wind. Then finally the haunted ship sails down the navigable canal or river and out to sea: aboard is the Count in pursuit of his boy. When they open his coffin a dozen rats plop out of the dirt and slink and bite the seamen on the ankles (how they ever filmed this I'll never know, great big rats). . . The whole scene on the ship testifies to the grandeur of the horror of Coleridge's Ancient Mariner. Of itself the schooner glides into the port of Bremen with all the crew dead. The sucked-out Captain is tied to his wheel. A disciple of the Count imprisoned in a Bremen cell sees the schooner glide right by like a ghost and says: "The master is here!" Down cobbles deserted at dusk suddenly, like an insane delivery boy here comes Count Nosferatu carrying his own coffin of burial earth under his arm. He goes straight to establish residence in an eerie awful warehouse or armory which made me think: "I shall never go to Bremen if they have things like that! Armories with empty windows! Ow!"

The old Bremen lamplighter is aware of the foolish hallucinations of Bremen folk but he also looks scared as he lights the evening lamp, naturally, as the next day processions carry the coffined victims of the vampire down the gloomy street. People close their shutters. There is real evil swarming all over the screen by now. Nosferatu looks worse and worse: by now his teeth are stained, his fingernails are like rats' tails, his eyes are on fire. He stares from his warehouse window like someone in an old dream. He rises from his coffin at eve like a plank. His disciple who escapes from the prison looks like Mr. Pickwick on a rampage in a chase that has everybody breathing furiously (a masterpiece of breathing), ends in a field, with torches.

At night, by moonlight there he is, the Great Lover, staring across that awful plaza or canal into the heroine's window and into her eye. She waits for him. She wants to save the hero and has read in the "Book of Vampires" that if a victim stays with the vampire till cock's crow he will be destroyed. He comes to her swiftly with that awful quickfooted walk, fingernails dripping. The shadow of the hand crawls like ink across her snowy bedspreads. The last scene shows him kneeling at her bedside kissing into her neck in a horribly perverted love scene unequalled for its pathetic sudden revelation of the vampire's essential helplessness. The sun comes up, you see its rays light the top of his warehouse, the cock crows, he can't get away. He vanishes in a puff of smoke like the Agony of the West. Right there on the floor as the puffing hero arrives too late to save his love.

The creator of this picture, F. W. Murnau, may have drawn a lot of information from the great vampire dissertations of Ranft and Calmet written in the 18th century. Vampire is a word of Servian origin (Wampir), — meaning blood-sucking ghosts. They were supposed to be the souls of dead wizards and witches and suicides and victims of homicide and the Banished! (those banished from family or church). But vampires were also thought to be the souls of ordinary living people which leave the body in sleep and come upon other sleepers in the form of down-fluff! . . . so don't sleep in your duck-down sleepingbag in Transylvania! (or even in California, they say).

Actually, don't worrry . . . scientifically speaking, the only blood-sucking bats in the world are located in South America from Oaxaca on down.

On Sports

Ronnie on the Mound

During infield practice the Chryslers are out on the field in their golden-yellow uniforms and the warm-up pitcher is little Theo K. Vance, bespectacled and scholarly, testing out his blazing fireball at catcher Babe Blagden, the veteran of more years in the league than he'd care to admit to any babe he tried to pick up last night in the Loop — it's a spring night in Chicago, the occasion a crucial game between the Chicago Chryslers (tied for the league lead with St. Louis at 21-11 all) and the Pittsburgh Plymouths, the usual door mats of the league now rejuvenated not only with a new manager, old Pie Tibbs an all-time all-star great centerfielder and slugger, but with new additions like the kid outfielder Oboy Roy Turner, the steady rookie Leo Sawyer at short (son of veteran Vic Sawyer) and their new star pitcher Ronnie Melaney just up from the minors with a dazzling record and rumors of a blazing fast ball. It's May in the Loop town, the wind blows softly from the lake, with a shade of autumnal coolness in the air presaging the World Series excitement to come, even the lowly Plymouths at a 14-won and 18-lost record hoping to be up there by that time now that they have that new wild line-up — but it's just really another game, another night, the usual gathering, cigar smoke in the stands, hot dogs, the call of beer sellers, the latecoming fans, the kids yelling in the bleachers (Friday night) and the old umpire like W. C. Fields in black coat and bursting pants bending to brush the plate as on a thousand other occasions in his old spittoon life — but the thrill runs through the crowd to see the rookie making his debut on the big-league mound: Ronny Melaney, nineteen, handsome, with dark eyes, pale skin, nervous hands, rubbing his hands down his green-striped trousers, kicking the mound, handling the resin bag and eyeing the bright lamps all around the stadium, newspapermen in the press box leaning forward to report his showing. Old Frank "Pie" Tibbs is out there on the mound giving Ronnie last-minute pats on the pants. "Take it easy kid, these Chryslers can be beat just like the bushwallopers back home." "Thanks, Mr. Tibbs," gulps Ronnie as he takes a step off the mound and pretends to fiddle with his shoes as the umpire calls "Batter up" and the stands vibrate with the excitement of the opening pitch of the game. The first batter will be Lefty Murphree the new sensation, called a "sophomore," in his second year of play with the Chryslers, whose speed (16 doubles) and general .300 hitting has skyrocketed the Chryslers up to top tie position, a murderous hitter, second in the league also in stolen bases with 9 (behind the incomparable Pancho Villa of Los Angeles), a left-handed beauty, stepping in now with a delicate pinch at his cap tip and a knock on his spikes and a spit to the side, as the old umpire handles his bellywhomper and straightens it out and prepares to half squat to squint at that pitch and call 'em straight. Now Murphree is in the box leveling his bat around in easy aiming strokes and is the first big-leaguer to be looking down the slot at Ronnie Melaney.

The sign is for a fast ball. *Let 'em see it, boy!* thinks the catcher (antique Jake Guewa of thirty years on the very same Pittsburgh team — a hard, browned, seamy little man with guts of iron, a weak hitter but a clutch hitter, who maybe after six games hitless and arid can suddenly win a game with an unobtrusive single in the bottom of the ninth). "Come on Daddy Kid!" Ronnie dangles the ball from his strong right hand, nods, steps on the rubber, winds back and forth a little rock, throws up the left leg, comes around like a whip and balls one in straight at Murphree's strike zone and Murphree swings a mean white bat and the ball whistles past the umpire's crowned noggin for a bang-in foul strike into the screen and umpire J. C. Gwynn raises right hand and shouts "Streeike!" and the game is on and the crowd goes "Whooee!"

Old Jake Guewa takes a peak at the bench and Manager Pie Tibbs gives him the sign for a curve; Ronnie's curve is a good one with a hopper, many's the old seamed scout watched it from behind the screen in the Texas League. Ronnie nods and gulps, he likes to concentrate on his fast ball, but orders are orders. He winds back and forth as a gust of wind comes and ripples the flags around the stadium, someone whistles, someone hoots and the white pellet is seen flying home high in the night toward the tense Murphree — the umpire throws up his left arm, yells, "Ball one" and the crowd goes, "Oh, oh." Guewa has the ball where it exploded *plow* into his glove, holds it aloft as such, walks a few feet ahead of the plate, says something to Ronnie, who strains to listen and comes forward a few steps. Guewa fires it at him, hard, as if to wake him up, turns and goes back with the inestimable sorrow of the baseball catcher to squat and as if to sigh again behind that old plate and Murphree knocks the spikes with the bat (one and one is the count, the kid's first major-league count), grits his teeth, sets that foot back on the rubber and sees the sign for fast ball and says to himself, *I'll burn this guy right down!* and whams it around, wild and high again. "Ball Two!" "Hey!" yells the crowd. "He's wild!" "Throw the bum out!" "Where'd you get the bushman!" "Come on, kid, settle down!" "He's got fire in that ball but we better call the fire dee-part-ment": laughter, discussion, conversation between women about how cute he is, kids yelling with glee about nothing they can understand, a bottle breaking somewhere far back in the johns. Melaney is behind in the count and now he begins to sweat and takes the sign for sinker and nods gravely — he's afraid to look toward the bench where maybe now Manager Tibbs is frowning. Murphree strands in there, leveling the bat around, careful as a hawk, eyes right on Ronnie, chewing with no feeling. Ronnie winds up and delivers with his heart as big as a toad: strike down the middle which Murphree only glances at, because he's had his own orders to let this one go by — the ball has come in high, like a vision, but sunk in across the chest perfectly spotted, landing in old Guewa's glove like a shot of a gun, *plow!* "Yay!" yells a fan. "He'll make it! You'll be awright baby!" And now the count is two and two and Jake gives the sign for a fast ball, Ronnie steels himself, remembers the calm with which he used to deliver pitches like this on drowsy afternoons in Dallas and Fort Worth and even before that in the Sunset League in Arizona, and in a dream he lets go his next pitch, high, too high, just off, ball three! And now it's a full count.

Manager Pie Tibbs is staring anxiously toward the mound, trying to think what to order; finally he sends the sign to the catcher, curve ball, who transmits it to Ronnie, who gulps because a curve ball is harder to control — *But I'll make it true!* There is a silence now in the stadium, you can hear little clicks of teletypes up in the press box, and small familiar sounds like a distant car horn in the street, and the usual whistles and catcalls: "He's a bum left, let 'im have it!" "Another two-bagger, boy!" (These cries are from the Chrysler bench, from Hophead Deane the crazy first-baseman and from utility men like Ernie Shaw and veteran Johnny Keggs and kids like Phil Drayton the speed-boy pinch runner.) Ronnie winds up now and lets her go at Lefty Murphree, who's ready and raps the bat around and connects with a dead knock that signifies he's topped the ball and it bounces down in front of him and goes skittering straight at first-baseman Wade Hazard who just stands as if knock-kneed to let it pop into his glove and if he misses with the glove the knees'll stop it; it sticks in his glove and nonchalantly (almost spitting) he straightens up and trots to the first-base bag well ahead of the racing, smoky Murphree, out, and Murphree streaks across the bag a dead pigeon and Ronnie Melaney's first man up has grounded out to first.

But here comes mighty Herb Jangraw to the plate; a second ago he was kneeling and spitting with three bats between his big mitts, dreaming of something else, waiting for his turn, now here he comes for his licks and it's only the beginning of Ronnie Melaney's career in the world. The crowd lets out a yowl of joy to see the old-time great slugger in a slump this year, but still as explosive as ever potentially, a man who has hit home runs out of sight in every ball park in the league, six-foot-four, 210 pounds, a rangy body, mighty arms, a great, ragged, ruinous face — drinks cases of beer by himself, a big jaw, a big cud, a big splurt of brown tobacco juice on the green fresh grass, he doesn't care, hitches his mighty pants and steps in, also left-handed, but with an immense long 45-inch bat that puts the fear of God into Ronnie to see it. "Phew," says the kid — only one out and two to go, and then only one inning and eight to go, and then only one game and thirty, forty for the year, and then only one year and twenty to go (if lucky) and then death O Lord. Jake Guewa steps out a ways, winks at Ronnie, gives him the sign for a sinker, goes back and squats; the old umpire leans in, Ronnie toes the rubber, rocks, rocks one time extry, throws up the left leg and burns one down, twisting his wrist as hard as he can to make that sinker *sink* dear God or Jangraw'll golf it out of sight and Pittsburgh. He does golf it, hits it with a woodsy whack, it goes arcing weakly to the left, the third-baseman Joe Martin makes a leap but it means nothing, he knows he can't get it, he even lets his good glove go as a sign of *O well;* the glove sails up and the ball sails out to left field, where Oboy Roy scutters up to recover it and fires it to second at little Homer Landry, as Jangraw gallumps down to first and makes a halfhearted turn and goes back to stand on the bag with a single to left, arms akimbo and spitting brown juice and nodding as Wade Hazard makes a smiling remark at him and the first-base umpire yells some joke and the fans are buzzing and sitting down again. But what now? What with the next batter, the mighty Babe Blagden, one of the greatest hitters of all time and currently batting .323 — in only 29 games he's had 31 hits and already delivered 8 homers (3 behind Jangraw) and catching up to the league leaders after he'd originally decided (in the spring) to give up active playing and be a coach, then persuaded to pinch hit, which he did with three home runs in a row or so, and so now back in the regular lineup and booming as good as ever.

Now Manager Pie Tibbs is stalking up and down before the bench with that familiar walk of his, well-known to two generations of baseball fans, that cat stalk, only now there are lines in his face and he has to decide weighty issues. The fans are jeering Ronnie, "It's only the beginning kiddo!" "Let's see that famous fast ball, Babe loves that fast ball!" "Beer! get me cold beer!" A cold sweat is on Ronnie's brow, he wipes it away like grease, he rubs his hands in the sand, on the resin bag, something's wrong with his body juices — *I've gotta get outa this inning!* he prays — he gets the sign and gets ready to deliver.

It's a fast ball, fast as he can make it, to catch Blagden off balance; Babe is a right-hand powerhouse and swings with his wrists alone. He likes it and steps in with a short dusty push of his cleated foot and toothpicks the bat around and clacks it a weak popup into the air off the mound which Ronnie himself takes with a reassuring hand wave to the others. "I got it," he calls.

So Jangraw is left standing on first base and now there's two outs and can Ronnie make it? Babyface Kolek, the recent hot hitter of the league rewarded with cleanup spot on the Chryslers, is stepping in and the stands are in an uproar. Kolek is such a clever clutchhitter Manager Pie Tibbs is worried and comes out to the mound to talk to Ronnie; Pie is also worried about the kid's debut, his beginning inning will be so important in his development, besides who wants Jangraw sent around from first to score and put the Chryslers out ahead in the first inning.

"Boy, I want you to take it cagey with this Kiolex, he's a mean little bastat, let him have an assortment, start with a curve and keep it outside." "Yessir, Mr. Tibbs." "Lissen, kid, I don't have to come out here in the first inning, but I notice you're nervous . . . let old Jake tell you what to do now, aim straight." Ronnie, in a dream, toes the rubber, eyes Jangraw leading off first. Pie is back in the dugout, sitting, hunched, watching, Ronnie pumps fast and pours her in, at the left-handed, squatting, keen-eyed Kolek, who lets it by his letters for a perfect strike. "Two more boy!" yells Jake Guewa, whanging the ball back, smarting Ronnie's hand. He pours another one in high, the count is even and still in the balance — "Just a few more pitches!" He sweats . . . now he pauses, wipes his hands, wishes for a drink of water, or a Coke, swallows, takes the sign for change-of-pace fast ball and again checks on big Jangraw on first, with Wade Hazard hovering behind him, both doing a little, slow, big-man hop. Ronnie turns his face from them and his arm responds, hard, whiplash, down-the-wrist twists, the ball sails home, sinks too far, low, for ball two — "What's the matter with me! Do I have to do everything in this world?" "Come on, kid!" yells the old third-base coach Pep McDill who's been with the Plymouths since the beginning of time, now a bowlegged pot-bellied old-timer with no real cares but plenty of sympathy, whom Ronnie as a kid had seen skittering around short-stop in Pittsburgh like a little rabbit. Sighing, Ronnie does the fast rock and comes in with his sinker, Kolek's eyes light up and he lunges for it, his right foot shows the cleated sole, Ronnie sees the bat come around and blinks as it explodes hard and whistles over his head and into center field where Tommy Turner is running like a smooth hare to recover and whip it on down to third, after some difficulty, and even slow-footed Jangraw has made it to there on the long single and there are men on first and third and two out and things are tight.

O Lord, thinks Ronnie, *I'll get the boot sure, starting off like this!* Manager Pie Tibbs looks for the first time toward the bull pen in left field, this he's never done before. *That's the sign*, thinks Ronnie, his heart sinking. *Another boner and I'm out in the showers.* It will be K. L. Jordan facing him, bespectacled, bookkeeperish thin, but one of the most consistent hitters in baseball, currently whacking .307 in 32 games, with a slew of clutch hits to his credit, a dangerous man, the whole Chicago line-up packed with enthusiastic dynamite. Jake Guewa gives the sign for fast ball, Jordan's weakness; it will be a case of burn him down. Ronnie eyes the men on first and third one after the other, pauses, the whole game hinges on his action, and he blows her in and Jordan likes it and easily, with an expression of glint in his spectacles though there is unconcern on the face itself, and placks it down on the grass where again it rolls to Wade Hazard at first who leaps, startled to see it, and goes over a few feet and takes it in and trots a few feet to first and steps on the bag, sealing Ronnie's courage into the records — and Ronnie slowly walks off the mound, letting off a big sigh that can be seen deflating his chest from the farthest gloomiest seat in the upper deep center-field bleachers, and as he does he takes one side look of longing at his wife in the stands and she holds up her fingers in the sign of "All straight" and Ronnie is made.

Three for the St. Petersburg *Independent*

In Mid-June My Ideas About the Major League Race

ST. PETERSBURG, FLA. (Independent) June 16, 1965 — This old sorry horse will now predict the end of the pennant race, and lay it on the line on a 5 cent bet with the thousands of eager fans who will challenge me no bout contest.

You guys better look out for the Detroit Tigers. Mickey Lolich, Dave Wickersham, Hank Aguirre and some other kidneys ah caint remember are good pitchers: but the main thing is: Don Demeter at first base, a tall longball hitter, the great Al Kaline (perennial bonus boy and destined for the Hall of Fame), Norm Cash! a great favorite among solid Detroit lovers of good hitting, even Jake Wood lately sick, (to come back), and not that I can't finish a sentence but there's Willie Horton currently leading the league in hitting, and the grand rookies (they are the ones who make all the difference); Jim Northrup and George Thomas: and lastly, not least to mention, and the true measure of the Tigers, Dick McAuliffe (a name I'm proud to type down) and Jerry Lumpe. There you've got your infield, your outfield, your pitching staff, and the catcher is another future hall-of-famer Bill Freehan. Let us watch that for gas.

My bet is now five dollars.

In the National League I pick the Milwaukee Braves. Rico Carty makes the difference, with the greatest living ballplayer Hank Aaron at his side, and then add Mac Jones, the Hall of Fame Eddie Mathews (right among us now), and pitchers like Cloninger, the enormous power and precision of that lineup: Joe Torre the best catcher since Roy Campanella and not only because he also has a Spanish name. The Milwaukee Braves, if the pitching holds up, have the power to DOWN anybody in the National League. Franchises have nothing to do with this. Simple baseball is beautifully played before people. As Dizzy (Jerome Hanna) Dean says "Aint nothin I like better than a good ball game." Every American is interlocked with Cooperstown. (Look out for the Dodgers in the National, and the Yanks in the American.)

The Greatest Sports Writers Who Ever Lived as Far as I'm concerned

ST. PETERSBURG, FLA. (Independent) July 10, 1965 — As for me, it was Dan Parker. I never thought Jimmy Cannon was so hot as he thought he was because of all his dismal attempts at trying to sound like Hemingway, or like Runyon, or rather he was trying to sound like somebody's avant garde idea of what a sportswriter should sound like if he were (or was) really smart. Jimmy Cannon I read with avid interest, but for information I go to Frank Graham and Dan Parker and Red Smith ain't bad and James Daley purty good. Now you know I can spell but so many of us spend our time reading sports pages we might as well for once start talking about the quality of our sportswriters. I don't wish to knock Jimmy Cannon. But please pay attention, will you, to the old *Daily Mirror* columns of Dan Parker and put them together in a book. Frank Graham had a sparse, thin-as-a-rail style that appealed to me simply as reportage devoid of style-consciousness and yet conscious of the quality of what prose should be. This may sound too silly to readers of sports pages but it's true.

Dan Parker was the dean of American sportswriters

because he wrote a long column every night, using dialects which were Italian, Jewish, Greek, French-Canadian, Irish, Polish but he could never master the Okie accent. My father, an old printer, used to read him with massive delight and I mean massive. He drew my attention to Dan Parker. After Dan Parker there can be no sportswriter in America. Let's just call this a little eulogy to Dan Parker's genius. (Am I allowed this, James Wechsler, Editor of the New York *Post*, where some great new sportswriters are working?) (And there's Stan Isaacs of the Long Island paper *Newsday*, excellent.) As for Grantland Rice, that belongs to the Thomas Wolfe period of American sportswriting.

I could go on into a long story about Clem McCarthy, the radio announcer but let the Monaghans, the O'Reillys, the Cassidys, the McInerneys and the Kerwicks laugh awhile about that.

What Was the Punch That Knocked Out Liston?

ST. PETERSBURG, FLA. (Independent) July 10, 1965 — Somebody said it was a Karate punch, somebody said Liston flopped for money, somebody said it was a hard punch. Muhammad Ali said it was a "surprise" punch he'd been laying up, and some said it was whatever. Somebody here in the office said it was a "six-inch Twist." And somebody else said he didn't know what it was but he floored him.

Robert Goulet forgot the words to the National Anthem because he was probably having a big time with the French-Canadians of Lewiston, Maine, where an aunt of mine lives. The referee was that great fighter: Jersey Joe Walcott. Joe Louis, the Left Jab Champ, said he couldn't understand what happened. The eyes of all men in the world were on that fight. All men are interested in the World Heavyweight

Boxing championship fight. The mayor of the town was only in his thirties. From the Maine woods maybe a couple of old-timers came in, in Jeeps, after a snowshoe trek, to see the oldtime American cigar-smoke fight scene. It was all over. Everybody thought it was mysterious. In the old days there was nothing mysterious about Carnera hitting Schaaf. I have no right to write this because I wasn't there. But the Clay-(Muhammad Ali)-Floyd Patterson fight is coming up sometime and once again men all over the world will be interested. Every man in the world had to put up his dukes at one time or another, or refused to (as Jesus refused to), but it's always interesting because it's so personal, immediate no-bull-allowed. A good prizefighter, because with gloves, is still Christianly legal. And remember that they started without gloves: John L. Sullivan, James Corbett, Sam Langford . . .

I may be whistlin' thru Dixie, but I'd rather see a Heavyweight Boxing Championship fight than a P.G.A. anyday. (Golf being long distance pool.) (Jack Nicklaus forgive me.) You can bet your life: boxing matches are sad, and everything is sad anyhow, till that day when the Lion lies down with the Lamb.

In the Ring

My jewel center of interest when I think of sports as is, or as we say in the academic circles, *per se*, which means "as is" in Latin, is that sight I had one time of a young teen-age boxer hurrying down the street with a small blue bag in which all his fundamental things were packed: jockstrap I guess (I know), trunks, liniment, toothbrush, money, vitamin pills mayhap, T-shirts, sweat shirt, mouthpiece for all I know, under the grimly drab lamps of New England on a winter night on his way to, say, Lewiston Maine for a semifinal lightweight bout for 10 bucks a throw for all I know, or for (O worse!) Worcester Massachusetts or Portland Maine, or Laconia N. H., to the Greyhound or Trailways bus a-hurrying and where his father is I'll never have known, or his mother in what gray tenement, or his sister or brothers in what war and lounge — with a nose not yet broken, and luminous eyes, and meaningful glance at the sidewalk 'pon which he pounds to his destination the likes of which, whatever it ever became, shall never be visited on any angel that was fallen from heaven — I mean it, what's the sense of knocking your brains out for a few bucks? — I saw this guy outside the little training gym my father ran in Centerville, Lowell Mass., about 1930, when he first introduced me to sports by taking me in there to watch the boys hammer away at punching bags and big sandbags, and if you ever see an amateur heavyweight whacking away fullfisted at a sandbag and making the whole gym creak, you'll learn never to start a fight with any big boy you ever do meet in any bar from Portland Maine to Portland Oregon — And the young pug's name on the street was probably Bobby Sweet.

I was 8 at the time and soon after that my big fat cigarsmoking Pa (a printer by trade) had turned the place into a wrestling club, organization, gymnasium, and promotion, call it what you will, but the same guys who were boxers the year before were now wrestlers; especially old Roland Bouthelier, who was my father's unofficial chauffeur 'cause my father couldn't drive his 1929 Ford himself his legs being too short, or him having to try to talk too much while driving, and Roland being also a young friend of the family's (about 22) and a worker in his printing plant to boot — Now Roland was a wrestler and my sister Nin (10) and I always beseeched him to show us his muscles when he came in the house for occasional supper and certainly for holiday suppers and he always obliged and Nin hung from one biceps and I hung from the other, whee . . . What a build! Like Mister America. One time he swallowed his tongue and almost choked at Salisbury Beach. He had a touch of epilepsy. During his youth there, my father was his friend and employer and protector. No capitalism involved, as tho a two-bit wrestling promoter and a one-bit printer could be a capitalist in a city of 100,000 people and him as honest as the day pretended to be long.

So I remember the time in about 1931 when I heard Roland being given sincere instructions in a dressing room smelling of big men sweat and liniment and all the damp smells that come from the showers and the open windows, "Go out there etc.," and out comes me and my Pa and we sit right at ringside, he lights up his usual 7-20-4 or Dexter cigar, the first match is on, his own promoted match, it's Roland Bouthelier against wild Mad Turk McGoo of the Lower Highlands and they come out and face each other; they lean over and clap big arms and hands over each other's necks and start mauling around and pretty soon one of them makes a big move and knocks the other guy down on the soft hollowly bouncing canvas, "Ugh, OO," he's got a headlock around Roland's head with his big disgusting legs full of hair, I can see Roland's face (my hero) turn red, he struggles there, but the guy squeezes harder and harder. This was before wrestling matches had begun to be fixed? you say? Well Roland had just got his instructions to lose the match in the first minute and then in the next minute if possible, to make time for the semifinal and the main match. But I saw his face turn red with French-Canadian rage and he suddenly threw his legs out and shot himself out of the leg hold and landed on his behind and leaped up in one acrobatic move on his feet, turned, and took the Turk by the shoulders and shoved him against the ropes, and when the Turk bounced back he had him direct in the stomach with a Gus Sonnenberg head charge and knocked the guy so hard back against the ropes the ropes gave and the guy tilted over and landed at some used cigars under the apron of the ring, where he lay gazing up with bleary nonunderstanding eyes. So naturally the referee gives the count, slow as he can, but that guy is slow coming back in; as soon as he crawls thru the ropes Roland's got him by the neck and throws him over his shoulder, the poor guy lands slam on his back, Roland's on top of him and pins his two shoulders down, but the guy wriggles out and Roland falls on his behind, clips him with his two sneakered feet, knocks him over on his stomach, jumps on his back, gives him the Full Nelson (which means both arms under the other guy's armpits and twined around to join at the neck), makes him hurt and weep and cry and curse and wince awhile, then, with one imperious angry shove, knocks him over again to his back (one big biceped arm) and pins his two shoulders down and he's gone and thrown the match, so to speak, which he was supposed to lose, out of angry real wrestling fury.

I'm even in the showers afterward listening to my Pa and the men give Roland hell for making them lose all that money, Roland says simply, "OK but he spit in my face in the leg lock when he had me down there, I wont take that from nobody."

A week later Roland is driving me and Pa, my ma and my sister to Montreal Canada for a big Fourth of July weekend where Roland is going to be introduced to the most beautiful little French dolls in town, my elder cousin girls. He turns and looks at me in the back seat as we're passing Lake Champlain, yells in French, "Are you still there, Ti Pousse?" (Lil Thumb?)

About this time too my Pa takes me and my ma to see every big wrestling match which happened at the time (don't ask my why, except Lowell must have been a big wrestling town) between the two world champs, Gus Sonnenberg of Topsfield (or thereabouts Massachusetts, originally from Germany) and the great Henri DeGlane, world's champion from France — In those days wrestling was still for keeps, dont you see — In the first fall Gus Sonnenberg rushes off the ropes with a bounce and does his famous head-into-belly rush that knocks DeGlane right over the ropes upside down bouncing and into my mother's lap . . . He is abashed, says, "I'm sorry, Madame," she says, "I dont mind as long as it's a good French man." Then on the next play he pins Sonnenberg down with his famous leg stranglehold and wins the first fall. Later on, in the incredible cigarsmoke which always made me wonder how those guys could even breathe let alone wrestle (in the Crescent Rink in Lowell) somebody applies a wrenching awful hellish leg-spreading hold that makes some people rush home in fear and somebody wins, I forget who.

It was only shortly after that that wrestling matches began to be fixed.

Meanwhile in this Crescent there were boxing matches and what I liked, besides the action, and since I didnt gamble, being 10 and not caring about money bets then as even now, I saw some marvelous aesthetical nuances connected with indoor fight sports: heard: smelled the cigarsmoke, the hollow cries, the poem of it all . . . (which I wont go into just now).

Because now there's no time for poetry anyway. The only way to organize what you're going to say about anything is to organize it on a grand and emotional scale based on the way you've felt about life all along. Only recently, now at age 45, I saw I swear the selfsame young pug with the sad blue bag a-hurrying to the bus station in Massachusetts to make his way to Maine for another dreary prelim bout, with no hope now but maybe 50 bucks, and maybe a broken nose, but why should a young man do things like that and wind up in the bottom pages of smalltown newspapers where they always have the UPI or AP reports of fights: "Manila, Philippines, Jose Ortega, 123, of San Juan Puerto Rico, outpointed Sam Vreska, 121, Kearney, Nebraska, in ten rounds. . . . Hungry Kelly, 168, Omaha, Nebraska, kayoed Ross Raymond, 169, Ottawa, Canada, in round 2." You read those things and you wonder what makes them so eagerly helpless in the corner when their seconds are sponging their reddened nose. Well never expect me to go into the ring! I'm too yellow! Could it say in the lexicon of publishing stories that Grass Williams outpointed or kayoed Gray Glass in the fifth? in Beelzabur Town? I say, God bless young fighters, and now I'll take a rest and wait for my trainer's bottle, and my trainer's name is Johnny Walker.

Last Words

The Last Word
(Column for *Escapade* Magazine)

One   (June 1959)

My position in the current American literary scene is simply that I got sick and tired of the conventional English sentence which seemed to me so ironbound in its rules, so inadmissable with reference to the actual format of my mind as I had learned to probe it in the modern spirit of Freud and Jung, that I couldn't express myself through that form any more. How many sentences do you see in current novels that say, "The snow was on the ground, and it was difficult for the car to climb the hill"? By the childish device of taking what was originally two short sentences, and sticking in a comma with an "and," these great contemporary prose "craftsmen" think they have labored out a sentence. As far as I can see it is two short sets of imagery belonging to a much longer sentence the total imagery of which would finally say something we never heard before if the writer dared to utter it out.

Shame seems to be the key to repression in writing as well as in psychological malady. If you don't stick to what you first thought, and to the words the thought brought, what's the sense of bothering with it anyway, what's the sense of foisting your little lies on others? What I find to be really "stupefying in its unreadability" is this laborious and dreary lying called craft and revision by writers, and certainly recognized by the sharpest psychologists as sheer blockage of the mental spontaneous process known 2,500 years ago as "The Seven Streams of Swiftness."

Those who will answer *Escapade's* "The Beginning of Bop" letter contest (April issue) with disagreeing notes may be right, and I may be wrong, but it has been recorded in the

Surangama Sutra that Gotama Buddha did say "If you are now desirous of more perfectly understanding Supreme Enlightenment, you must learn to answer questions spontaneously with no recourse to discriminative thinking. For the Tathagatas (the Passers-Through) in the ten quarters of the universes, because of the straight-forwardness of their minds and the spontaneity of their mentations, have ever remained, from beginningless time to endless time, of one pure Suchness with the enlightening nature of pure Mind-Essence."

Which is pretty strange old news.

My opinion about current American literature is that the best of it has not been published yet. Only recently for instance have they begun to print some of William Seward Burroughs' huge *Naked Lunch*, a work that may prove repulsive to many, many people when they get to see it but in time will mellow in their minds with the changing of the times into a soft song of human love (*Lolita's* nothing compared to it, de Sade pales). Some of it will mellow into a soft human song, that is, and the rest of it, the "reprehensible" part, will become known as highgrade American Humor in the great tradition, by the world's greatest living satirist. His language is Mid-American Missourian ("Motel Motel Motel loneliness moans across the continent like fog horns over still oily water tidal rivers").

A fabulous young American poet of the very first magnitude in the history of English is Gregory Corso, whose best long poems, *Bomb*, *Army*, *Marriage* and whole Mexicanas of notebooks of poetry he scribbled in Mexico have not been printed (and a lot of his best work he's personally rejected himself and hid under floorboards, and some he lost by the suitcaseful in buses!) ("O Atom Bomb, resound thy tanky knees!").

Allen Ginsberg's entire output since *Howl* and much of it before he hasn't even bothered to type up, let alone submit.

His work is evenly Ginsbergian, I like best his wild little notebooks in which he thinks he's "making notes" for future poems and instead the poems are there, perfect ("Max who doesn't swing as much but paints asiatic mandalas is here, also great crowd of new people, african sculpting paranoiac spades and one short glitter-eyed egyptian who blows bop is a poltroon & works in bodybuilding school teaching").

My own best prose has yet to be published, my *Visions* and *Dreams* and *Dharmas* — when I want a friend to enjoy my style I hand him these unpublished things but the editors have been reluctant to go all out and print these. ("Madroad driving men ahead, lonely, leading around the bend into the openings of space towards the horizon Wasatch snows promised us in the vision of the West, spine heights at the World's end, coast of blue Pacific starry night — nobone half-banana moons sloping in the tangled night sky, the torments of great formations in mist, the huddled invisible insect in the car racing onwards, illuminate.")

Poetry and prose rejects of people like Phil Whalen, Gary Snyder, Denise Levertov, Robert Creeley, in fact e.e. cummings, Auden, James Jones, Algren, etc. are probably the most interesting things in American Lit today yet editors have been sifting through writers' manuscripts for the rocks of fool's gold and letting the real gold dust drop. Editors and writers have been engaged on a campaign of systematic rejection of everything except the most systematic manuscripts. In fact, the notebook should come back, printed, and like in France the cheap paperback editions of a writer's entire collected works, notes and outcries and doodles-drawings and all. This would institute a literature of facts of life and writing, not of mere readability measurement — a rich *school* of writing, assisted by wise editors like Don Allen of *Evergreen Review* and Irving Rosenthal of *Chicago Review* and Leroi Jones, the emergence of something better than the novel (dead as the Victoria) and something better than fanciful versification, to be rejected as diarrhea of the mouth for fifty years by critics but accepted and enjoyed as unabashed language by *readers*.

Two (July 1959)

Who told Willy Mays to change his batting stance from 1951 straight-in-the-box upright honest to the now-crouch business with back knee bent so that he can no longer clobber outside pitches and put the meat part of the bat flush on the seamless noggin of the base ball and drill it down the third base line? Know-it-alls!

Who told Karl Spooner to get operated, ruining one of the greatest pitching prospects of all time, right after he struck out seventeen men in his major league debut, all this stuff about bone-chips and about knives being stuck into the hard muscular arms of pitchers?

Why doesn't somebody tell Early Wynn how to cure his phlebitis by standing on his head three minutes a day against a wall, then he'd have five great years left in him?

How can anybody ever beat Hornsby's and Lafoie's batting records with all that silly trickery of the Boudreau Shift? Is that honest baseball, to swing the infield over to catch a pull hitter's advantage and make of it little with a Schoendienst glove?

How can anybody ever break Babe Ruth's homerun record with all these silly intentional walks? As soon as a guy starts to hit homeruns he's on base every minute.

What better hit-and-run than a good smacking triple?

Why has the prerogative of figuring out a pitcher been transferred to coaches and managers who give hand-signs and ruin the game with their deleterious and vicarious master-minding?

Why is beautiful Ted Williams always booed by stupid Boston crowds and abused by sportswriters just because he doesn't care what people think of him and his big salary or how jealous they are about his winning batting titles year after year or the fact that he wants to go fishing in Florida and is like young Ernest Hemingway? Was Ty Cobb treated that badly?

Why didn't Casey Stengel start Bob Turley in the last game of the 1958 World Series and only put him in after a million fans sent him telepathic messages?

Who wants to hoodoo all the young greats with the sophomore jinx except jealous people? It's like someone sneezing and you tell them they must have Asian Flu instead of telling them to sniff Dristan and cool it.

Humorous note: how comes it that when somebody like Ted Williams, left handed, sliding his hands up and down the ash blond bat then gripping it with Syrian intensity sometimes with tapes on his wrists and adjusts his wide stance in the box and holds ready and when the pitch comes in unfinishes the symphony of the southpaw's disdain with a mad screaming linedrive homerun into the rightfield bleachers where people duck, always there's one mad fan who stands and catches the ball barehanded which is a feat that even the ballplayers themselves couldn't do?

Why can't the Little Leaguers just play baseball without being pestered and supervised and prevented from becoming juvenile delinquents by dreary supervisory coaches who should try the delinquent ministry?

Why are natural pull hitters taught to hit to the other field? By castrated thinkers?

Why is so much fuss made about owners and managers and general managers and general batboys? Supposing you had to sit around all day reading about the photographers of beautiful girls in *Escapade* instead of seeing the girls themselves?

Why do guys who tool bats all winter long in their cellar and follow the hotstove league, come out in spring managing teams in the mist and always insist on the hit-and-run from a third base coaching box? Why don't they dig the power of baseball in the very bats they tool?

And pitchers who learn to pitch against barn doors like Bob Feller should never be told how to throw a fast ball or a curve or any pitch any more than a natural brokenfield runner in football should be yelled at with megaphone when to dodge and when not to?

Everybody's trying to get into the act.

In the first inning of the first game of every World Series did you ever notice how all the ballplayers act with a huge slow motion burl of their arms and shoulders and legs, as though they were ballet dancers watched by the whole world?

How come the people who love baseball the most have never seen a World Series in the flesh and if they were offered the chance would rather listen to it on the radio or watch it on TV?

Why are so many shortstops called the greatest of all time and then immediately forgotten? Like Buddy Kern and Mr. Shortstop Marion? It must be that shortstop is the most controversial position in baseball.

What is the exact sound of bright new Louisville bats being thrown on the ground for batting practice, when they clunk together? Plank! Though the bats are loose and shiney do you know whether they are loose, do you wonder if the batter's hands are sweating and slipping at the bat handle or are they not, is the clean bat waved in waiting?

Why is third baseman so tragic? Why does the center fielder look dreamy in centerfield, hands on knees? Why is rightfielder bored looking? And leftfielder worried looking? And second baseman so neat looking, like an Irish Jesuit? Or first baseman always look like a tall Indian? Or the catcher like a man of responsibilities in a modern cigarette ad when he removes his shin guards?

Why does it give one so much joy to see burly fans bend eager elbows to their knees for the first pitch?

Let there be joy in baseball again, like in the days when Babe Ruth chased an enemy sportswriter down the streets of Boston and ended up getting drunk with him on the waterfront and came back the next day munching on hotdogs and boomed homeruns to the glory of God.

Three   (October 1959)

Because none of us want to think that the universe is a blank dream on account of our minds so we want *belief* and plenty names, we want lists of laws and a little bit of harrumph shouldersback separation from the faceless UGH of True Heaven, I see men now standing erect in bleaky fields waving earnest hands to explain, yet ghosts, pure naught ghosts — And even the great Chinese who've known so much for so long, will paint delicately on silk the Truth Cloud upper skies that lead off over rose-hump unbelievable mountains and crunchy trees, indefinable waterfalls of white, then the earthbound scraggle tree twisted to a rock, then, because Human Chinese, the little tiny figures of men on horseback lost in all that, usually leaving 8/10ths of the upper silk to scan th'unscannable Void — So I was wiser when I was younger after a bad love affair and sat in my lonely November room thinking: "It's all a big crrrock, I wanta die," and thinking: "The dead man's lips are pressed tasting death, as bitter as dry musk, but he might as well be tasting saccharine for all he knows," yet these thoughts didn't stand up to the Four Noble Truths as propounded by Buddha and which I memorized under a streetlamp in the cold wind of night:

(1)   All Life is Sorrowful
(2)   The Cause of Suffering is Ignorant Desire
(3)   The Suppression of Suffering Can Be Achieved
(4)   The Way is the Noble Eightfold Path
(which you might as well say is just as explicit in Bach's *Goldberg Variations*.)
Not knowing it could just as well be:
(1)   All Life is Joy
(2)   The Cause of Joy is Enlightened Desire
(3)   The Expansion of Joy Can Be Achieved
(4)   The Way is the Noble Eightfold Path
since what's the difference, in supreme reality, we are neither subject to suffering nor joy — Why not? — Because who says?

But it was Asvaghosha's incomparable phrase that hooked me on the true morphine of Buddha: "REPOSE BEYOND FATE" — because since life is nothing but a short vague dream encompassed round by flesh and tears, and the ways of men are the ways of death (if not now, eventually, you'll see), the ways of beautiful women such as those pictured in this magazine are eventually the ways of old age, and since nothing we do seems to go right in the end, goes sour, but no more sour than what Nature intends in need of sour fertilizer for continuers and continuees, "repose beyond fate" meant "rest beyond what happens to you," "give it up, sit, forget it, stop thinking," YOUR OWN PRIVATE MIND IS GREATER THAN ALL — So that my first meditation was a tremendous sensation of "When did I do this last?" (it seemed so natural so right) "Why didn't I do it before?" — And all things vanished, what was left was the United Stuff out of which all things appeared to be made of without being made into anything really, all things I then saw as unsubstantial trickery of the mind, furthermore it was already long gone out of sight, the liquid waterball earth a speck in sizeless spaces but O then —

But it *is* a bleary blank, how foreign to our sweet hopeful (some of us) natures are the blind worms that'll eat our beloved vitals, beloved hands, holy noses, remembered jaws, the flesh on us which burns before eyes in 70 years burns slow burn, just as impersonal as if a hydrogen bomb should blow up the whole earth in a second to scarring fireball as prophesied aplenty — That's why when I recently bent my lips to my beloved's neck it seemed ephemeral to think "Is it her neck? her real me-neck, my-neck?" because it isn't anybody's neck at all because nothing's there but imaginary concatenation of mind — So O the ecstasy of that first meditation when I closed my eyes and saw golden swarms of nothing, the true thing, the thus-ness of Creation — All of us pieces of the United Stuff rising up awhile in shroudy form, to wave a minute (70 years among the myriad mindless multibillions), *bling*, mine-less neck lovely human beings and all the animals and insects and otherplanet creatures thinking they have a true SELF somewhere somehow in this sea of gold naught — Dust takes a flyer, then folds under, as flighty as a baby twister in the Pecos Plains of Texas you see across the sand swirling to no eyes, by nightfall where did it go? — Clap hands, lovely Buddha!

In my ancient books I read about Bodhisattva who said: "All living beings who discipline themselves in listening to Silence shall hear Heaven," (the blessedness that penetrates through appearances), "shall attain to the unattainable, shall enter the doorless, shall cross the river on the ferry and reach the other shore? and (no river, no ferry, no other shore) come New Year's Eve my mother and I toast martinis to each other and as she says "Happy New Year, dear boy, and I hope you'll be happy" and on the T.V. the horns and tootles are blowing (and in fleecy beds little boys wake up to hear the midnight bong below) I see that I *have* reached the other shore because it no longer matters to me about "happiness in this or any other world, "crossing the shore" has simply been the recognition that there's nothing to yearn after, nothing to think, my Essence of Mind, the universal One Sea of mysterious mentality, so that I raise a private toast to my mother and all beings (silently) wishing them the Sweet Dharma Truth instead of a Happy "New Year" — the sweet Dharma Truth, the unrecognizable recognition that which blots out (as snow blots out the blottable pitiful shapeliness of ogroid earth —

"The best lack all conviction," said Yeats, because as the ancient Chinese say: "He who knows does not speak."

Four   (December 1959)

Inside it is a perfect round bowl with a neat circle of brown dirt being harrowed and raked by expert loving rakers like the man who rakes second base in Yankee Stadium only this is Bite-the-Dust Stadium — When I sat down the bull had just come in and the orchestra was sitting down again — Fine embroidered clothes tightly fitted to boys behind a fence — Solemn they were, as a big beautiful shiny black bull rushed out gallumphing from a corner I hadn't looked, where he'd been apparently mooing for help, black nostrils and big white eyes and outspread horns, all chest no belly, stove polish thin legs seeking to drive the earth down with all that locomotive weight above — Some people sniggered — Bull galloped and flashed, you saw the riddled-up muscle holes in his perfect prize skin — Matador stepped out and invited and the bull charged and slammed in, matador sneered his cape, let pass the horns by his loins a foot or two, got the bull revolved around by cape, and walked away like Grandee — and stood his back to the dumb perfect bull who didn't charge like in *Blood & Sand* and lift Señor Grandee into the upper deck. Then business got underway. Out comes the old pirate horse with patch on eye, picador KNIGHT aboard with a lance, to come and dart a few slivers of steel in the bull's shoulderblade who responds by trying to lift the horse but the horse is mailed (thank God) — a historical and crazy scene except suddenly you realize the picador has started the bull on his interminable bleeding. The blinding of the poor bull in mindless vertigo is continued by the brave bowlegged little dart man carrying two darts with ribbon, here he comes head-on at the bull, the bull head-on for him, wham, no head-on crash for the dart man has stung with dart and darted away before you can say boo (& I did say boo), because a bull is hard to dodge. Good enough, but the darts now have the bull streaming with blood like Marlowe's Christ in the heavens — An old matador comes out and tests the bull with a few capes' turn then another set of darts, a battleflag now shining down the living breathing suffering bull's side and everybody *glad* — And now the bull's charge is just a stagger and so now the serious hero matador comes out for the kill as the orchestra goes one boom-lick on bass drum, it gets quiet like a cloud passing over the sun, you hear a drunkard's bottle smash a mile away in the cruel Spanish green aromatic countryside — Children pause over tortas — The bull stands in the sun head-bowed, panting for life, his sides actually *flapping* against his ribs, his shoulders barbed like San Sebastian — The careful footed matador youth, brave enough in his own right, approaches and curses and the bull rolls around and comes stoggling on wobbly feet at the red cape, dives in with blood streaming everywhichaway and the boy just accommodates him through the imaginary hoop and circles and hangs on tip-toe, knockkneed. And Lord, I didn't want to see his smooth tight belly ranted by no horn — He rippled his cape again at the bull who just stood there thinking "O why can't I go home?" and the matador moved closer and now the animal bunched tired legs to run but one leg slipped throwing up a cloud of dust — But he dove in and flounced off to rest — The matador draped his sword and called the humble bull with glazed eyes — The bull pricked his ears and didn't move — The matador's whole body stiffened like a board that shakes under the trample of many feet — A muscle showed in his stocking — Bull plunged a feeble three feet and turned in dust and the matador arched his back in front of him like a man leaning over a hot stove to reach for something on the other side and flipped his sword a yard deep into the bull's shoulderable separation — Matador walked one way, bull the other with sword to hilt and staggered, started to run, looked up with human surprise at the sky & sun, and then gargled — O go see it folks! — He threw up ten gallons of blood into the air and it splashed all over — He fell on his knees choking on his own blood and spewed and twisted his neck around and suddenly got floppy doll and his head blammed flat — He still wasn't dead, an extra idiot rushed out and knifed him with a wren-like dagger in the neck nerve and still the bull dug the sides of his poor mouth in the sand and chewed old blood — His eyes! O his eyes! — Idiots sniggered because the dagger did this, as though it would not — A team of hysterical horses were rushed out to chain and drag the bull away, they galloped off but the chain broke and the bull slid in dust like a dead fly kicked unconsciously by a foot — Off, off with him — He's gone, white eyes staring the last thing you see — Next bull! — First the old boys shovel blood in a wheel-barrow and rush off with it. The quiet raker returns with his rake — "Ole!," girls throwing flowers at the animal-murder in the fine britches — And I saw how everybody dies and nobody's going to care, I felt how awful it is to live just so you can die like a bull trapped in a screaming human ring —

Jai Alai, Mexico, Jai Alai!

Five   (February 1960)

The history of the world is bloody and sad and mad — The
First Crusade was nothing but Peter the Hermit spreading
the word and leading a ragged horde of unarmed poorfolk
who thought they could walk all the way to Jerusalem, Walter
the Penniless strode in front of them with a big long staff,
they never made it, they were all insane — Emperor
Frederick Barbarossa arrived at a river and wanted to show
his troops how to get across safely on horseback, so with all
his armor he spurred the horse into the stream and drowned
before their very eyes — The Children's Crusade was two little boys named Stephen of France and Nicholas of Germany
who wandered barefoot along the gray mist roads of
Medieval Europe gathering children to follow them and
ended up perishing in the snows of the Alps and what was
left of the pitiful ragged army was sold into slavery in
Mohammedan markets — Every phosphorescent fish in the
sea worries me like the Children's Crusade — History is a
vast inexplicable tale that seems to make no sense — The
Chalcedonian Patriarch of Alexandria was torn to pieces by a
crowd on Good Friday in his own church — Francis Bacon sat
in the snow with a dead chicken in his lap to prove the home
freezers of today but died of pneumonia — No wonder
Voltaire laughed ! — The Danes of the 8th Century were led
by King Harold Wartooth — Krum was the Khan of the
Bulgarians and Yah Yah the Sage of Baghdad — Harold
Fairhair killed Eric Bloodaxe on a big rock for reasons even
Ida Graymeadows'll never dream — In 896 the corpse of
Pope Formosus was propped up on a chair and put on trial —
Mazoria the Senatrix went to bed with Popes, gave birth to
Popes, and murdered Popes — At the Nicean and Chalcedon
Councils eastern priests sitting on both sides of the church
suddenly began screaming insane accusations across the holy

nave — The bones of John Wycliffe the first English translator of the Bible were dug up and burned — Huss burned a Papal Edict and himself was burned — Luther nailed the ninety-five Theses on the door of the Cathedral of Wittenberg and promptly married a nun while Henry the Eighth got mad at Luther in a political fit and joined the Roman Church but promptly broke from the Roman Church to marry Anne Boleyn but got sick of her too and cut off her head — Ancient sailors caught in enormous storms at sea were only afraid of Sea-monsters — Peter the Great the six-foot-nine giant Tsar of Russia executed people with his own hands — When Russia finally got enlightened Tsar Alexander II was assassinated by bomb-throwing nihilists — Later when a group of workers and a priest wanted a few words from the Tsar affectionately known as "The Little Father of All the Russias" they got rifle fire in the kisser — Catherine de Medici the Queen Mother of France threw a royal wedding at the church of St. Bartholomew and invited all the Huguenots and had them all massacred in their pews — The Thirty Years War was concluded by Richelieu who was jealous of the Hapsburgs and had many people killed for nothing, a Catholic Cardinal leading a Catholic country against a Catholic King and a Catholic Emperor all so's Richelieu can slaver his lips in midnight chambers — The early cure for fever was swallow a live spider in syrup — Semmelweiss was well-nigh crucified for suggesting that doctors wash their hands at childbirth — Man — Highest perfect fool, the wisdom of the two-legged rat — The great Habeas Corpus law was only passed in Parliament because a funny clerk decided to note down ten votes for a fat member of the House who weighed 350 pounds — John Randolph said that Edward Livingston "shines and stinks like rotten mackerel in the moonlight" and Napoleon called Talleyrand "a silk stocking full of mud" — Napoleon's soldiers crowded so hysterically around bonfires in the cold Russian winter that the nearest men were pushed in the fire and burned to death — The terrible war of 1870 was deliberately connived by Bismark who changed the wording of a peace telegram and during the Siege of Paris that followed Gambetta magnificently escaped in a BALLOON — The history of the world is full of olives. When the hell will people realize that all living beings whether human or animals, whether earthly or from other planets, are representatives of God, and that they should be treated as such, that all things whether living or inanimates and whether alive, dead, or unborn, and whether in the form of matter or empty space, are simply the body of God?

Six   (April 1960)

Intriguing thoughts about the Berlin Question — When President Roosevelt told General Eisenhower to hold up the rampaging American troops at the River Elbe line to allow the rampaging Russians to enter Berlin themselves, was he doing the big mad romantic shot of "letting the Russians taste the well deserved vengeance" because in his dream he saw them as suffering heroes (does this sound right?) (is that why Khrushchev laid a wreath on Roosevelt's tomb?), or was he in his innocent subconscious idealism actually setting up the conditions which have now ripened in the Berlin Crisis which gave Russia enough strength of position to bargain peacefully with a strong America thus paving the way (again via his unconscious idealistic victorious intuition or inspiration) to eventual world peace based on solid mutual strength (always subject to fluctuation however) — So what is the Berlin Crisis but this? And as to Pearl Harbor, is it true that a message was intercepted and hushed up so a war with Japan could be instituted? If that is so, the war was certainly going to begin a few minutes later with or without the message, or

was Roosevelt again dreaming idealistically but now with a
touch of madness and real madness at that, that nothing better could happen to America than a good solid awakening or
wake-up war with the Orient Power in order to bring the two
worlds of Wendell Willkie together, or was it just that a message came and somebody fumbled in human mistake mis-
coding it, or mis-hearing it, or was napping, or making the
secretary on the couch, or any number of human reasons,
Roosevelt himself smiling on his lawn not dreaming what's
happening, the usual confusion of the world of living beings.
You've got to be fair about these things, you never never
know anyway what's really happening in historic moments
(every detail) except for the hearsay you read in papers and it
half the time snidely twisted —

When Truman fired MacArthur was it because he really
believed that the General was mad and wanted to conquer
the world, being such a brilliant and powerful soldier and
statesman, or was Truman's reason simply rational having to
do with a genuine administration logistic State Department
midnight oil deliberation that the Korean War should not
extend beyond the Manchurian line — so that you think that
if Roosevelt was ignorant of power politics of real history in
giving Berlin to Stalin, or instinctively right in the long run
which we haven't seen yet, Truman was either pettish about
firing MacArthur and also concerned about what he under-
takes to think is Totalitarianism, or he took steps to reason
quietly peacefully with his best thinkers and they said
"MacArthur will ruin the logistic."

This proves I don't know anything about anything, one day
or the other you either have or want the great truth, but I do
know that human beings are confused almost hilariously so
everywhere and maybe history is based on confusion, like
when in football the T-Quarterback flips back the ball to the
right halfback who ain't there, or was there a second ago but

went running the other way (misjudged huddled instructions), the ball rolls, everybody's screaming, the left halfback
goes back and scoops it up, he starts running, they nail him
they think with a ten fifteen yard loss but he's snakily loose
and starts swinging way the other way around as everybody is
on their feet, you couldn't believe such a touchdown could
be possible but he goes all the way and upsets the
Conference Standings and newspapermen gasp, nobody
believes it, the Alumni President receives the news with a
stagger like a Prosecution Lawyer being whispered a new
development, newspapers are confused, the editor drowsing
over his editorial on the Berlin Crisis wakes up and says
"Wowp? I'll be hurt in time?"

Seven   (June 1960)

The American press is beginning to have a sow sorrowful
look about it — Last Fall I was watching Nikita Khrushchev
on TV as Eisenhower made his welcoming speech on the trip
from Moscow, and there was a hot sun shining down on the
Russian Premier's bald dome like a bulb you could see its
reflection on his frowning brow, so he put up his black hom-
burg hat against the glare and listened on to the speech —
and in the paper and on Television Newscasts of the free
American Press it said that Khrushchev was quick to immediately "upstage" the President the first chance he got and
immediately after proved this by referring to the Russian
moon-hit with a Russian pennant aboard which proved to
those arrogant looking commentators that he had raised his
hat to drown the dramatic significance of the other man's
speech — And I say this is a stinking lie against the man
Khrushchev standing there shielding his baldy brow from the
hot September sun (O Edgar Allan Poe, a school by your
name was bombed the same day by a maniac and the

Television news commentators gave this news also with great relish because they seemed to shine forth with great confident information that as long as things were bad they could keep their jobs) — And in the interest of keeping their jobs I say the American Press lies and lies in its teeth, because I had the same experience with them knowing the condition, the atmosphere, the joy and heart state of a handful of "beatnik" writers when they were knocking off their thesis back in the early Fifties before they were famous (and defamed) in the American Press — The smile of silence, the tenderness of scribbling by the lamp, the glee knowing what the American would learn from these words, and I know what the thing sounded like when *Time*, *Life*, TV and the paper reviewers were done depicting these artists as hoodlums, violents, cheerless wretches, drooling cretins, Clifton Fadiman showing a picture of me on TV with beard typing on a portable aboard a speeding motorcycle (never had either object), or the time I was on my way to the store with $90 to buy $5 worth of groceries and an $85 train ticket across the street at the station, and just as I hailed a bus a car stopped in front of me and two newspapermen told me to get on, they'd drive me to the store, which I didnt like because I wanted to be alone to think on the bus so I sat in their backseat pondering, adding a few words of greeting; and at the station I was $2 short on the train ticket (after the groceries) and borrowed $2 from the newspapermen — In the paper it said I had "condescended" somewhat grandiosely to be driven to the store and suddenly added "Hey I'm going to the grocery store and forgot my wallet, ha ha, how about lending me two dollars" (the Beatnik Bum, the Hobohemian of the Latrine, the chiseler, the tramp, the punk) — The American Press with its long face now, a bunch of mournful liars. That postprandial sissified form of flatulation.

I even saw a blatant lie in 1954 when Joe McCarthy made

one of his few brilliant points about increasing Communism in America and read the "full transcript" in the paper next day only to find it deleted — Now if I defend Khrushchev, Joe McCarthy and me that doesnt make me a Shmommunist but what is the matter with America when the time comes when men are so hung up on their jobs that they'll lie in public, in great numbers, under the mistaken assumption that "the news" has got to be bad, not good, or nobody will follow the news.

What happened to my contemporary, the robin, this morning, Henry David Thoreau?

Eight   (August 1960)

Travel isn't as good as it seems, it's only after you've come back from all the heat and horror that you forget to get bugged and remember the weird scenes you saw — In Morocco I went for a walk one beautiful cool sunny afternoon (with breeze from Gibraltar, I was in Tangiers) and my friend and I walked to the outskirts of the weird Arab town commenting on the architecture, the furniture, the people, the sky which he said would look green at nightfall and the quality of the food in the various restaurants around town, adding, he did, "Besides I'm just a hidden agent from another planet and the trouble is I don't know why they sent me, I've forgotten the god damn message dearies" so I says "I'm a messenger from Heaven too" and suddenly we saw a herd of sheep coming down the road and behind it an Arab shepherd boy of ten who held a little baby lamb in his arms and behind him came the mother lamb bleating and baa haa ing for him to take real good extry special care of the babe, which the boy said "Egraya fa y kapata katapatafataya" and spat it out of his throat in the way Semites speak — I said "Look a real shepherd boy carrying a baby lamb" and Bill said "O well, the little prigs are always rushing around carrying lambs." Then we walked down the hill to a place where a holy man or that is, a devout Mohammedan, knelt praying to the setting sun and Bill turned to me and said "Wouldn't it be wonderful if we were real American tourists and I suddenly rushed up with a camera to snap his picture" . . . then added . . . "by the way, how do we walk around him?"

"Around the right," I said.

We wended our way homeward to the chatty outdoor cafe where all the people gathered at nightfall beneath screaming trees of birds, near the Soco Grande, and decided to follow the railroad track. It was hot but the breeze was cool from the Mediterranean. We came to an old Arab hobo sitting on the rail of the track recounting the Koran to a bunch of raggedy children listening attentively or at least obediently. Behind them was their mother's house, a tin hut but the tin all painted the most beautiful pastel blue you ever saw in Cézanne or on the cover of *Escapade's* August 1959 issue — I didnt know what he was doing, I said "He's an idiot of some kind?" "No" says Bill "he's a wandering Sherifian pilgrim preaching the gospel of Allah to the children — they got some holy men in town that wear white robes and go around barefoot and dont let no bluejeaned hoodlums start a fight on the street, he just walks up and stares at them and they scat. Besides the people of Tangiers aint like the people of West Side New York, when there's a fight starts in the street among the Arab hoods all the men rush up out of *kief* parlors and beat the hell out of them. They aint got men in America any more, they just sit there and eat pizza before the Late Show, my dear." This man was William Seward Burroughs, the writer, and we were heading now down the narrow alleys of the Medina to a little bar and restaurant where all the Americans went. I wanted to tell somebody about the shepherd boy, the holy man and the man on the tracks but no one was interested. The big fat

Dutch owner of the bar said "I cant find a good poy in this town" (saying poy, not boy, but meaning boy) — Burroughs doubled up in laughter — We went from there to the late afternoon cafe where sat all the decayed aristocrats of America and Europe and a few eager enlightened healthy Arabs or near-Arabs or diplomats or whatever they were — I said to Bill "Where do I get a woman in this town?" (I had just arrived on a Yugoslavian freighter flying the big red star) — He said "There's a few whores that hang around, you have to know a cabdriver or something, or better than that there's a cat here in town, from Frisco, Jim, he'll show you what corner and what to do" so that night me and Jim the painter go out and stand on the corner and sure enough here come two veiled women, with delicate cotton veils over their mouths and halfway up their noses, just their dark eyes you see, and wearing long flowing robes and you see their shoes cuttin through the robes and Jim hailed a cab which was waiting there and off we went to the pad which was a patio affair with tile patio overlooking the sea and a Sherifian beacon that turned on and turned on, around and around, flashing in my window every now and again, as, alone with one of the mysterious shrouds, I watched her flip off the shroud and veil and saw standing there a perfect little Mexican (or that is to say Arab) beauty perfect and brown as October grapes (and maybe like the wood of Ebon) and turned to me with her lips parted in curious "Well what are you doing standing there?" so I lit a candle on my desk. When she left she went downstairs with me where some of my connections from Birmingham England and Morocco and U. S. A. were all blasting home-made pipes of "O" and singing Cab Calloway's old tune, "I'm gonna kick the gong around." On the street she was very polite when she got into the cab.

From there I went to Paris, where nothing was happening except the most beautiful girl in the world who didnt like my rucksack on my back and had a date with a guy with a small mustache who stands hand in sidepocket with a sneer in the nightclub movies of Paris.

Wow. And in London who do I see but a beautiful, a heavenly beautiful blonde standing against a wall in Soho calling out to well dressed men. Lots of makeup, with blue eye shadow, the most beautiful women in the world are definitely English . . . unless like me you like em dark.

Nine   (October 1960)

Zen is not letting yourself be horsewhipped into words about it so as you read these words just unfocus your eyes and stare at the blurry pages.

Zen is like a book called "This Existence" that starts off by saying "There are four things to do with this book, 1) Read it and keep it, 2) Read it and throw it away, 3) Dont read it and throw it away, 4) Dont read it and keep it. There are two final things to be done: 1) Stay away from it altogether, 2) Who said there was such a book called 'This Existence'?"

Zen is like staring at a word for several minutes until it entirely loses all its meaning, like you take the word SQUARE, look at it, look at that "Q," look at that "S" on one end and "E" on the other, and such silly combinations as "QUA" or "UARE" — Who invented it and what is the location of one's mind anyway?

Like that disciple who wanted to be enlightened so badly he cut his arm off and brought it to Bodhidharma who said "Why didnt you bring me your mind?" and the guy said "How can I tell where my mind is?" and Bodhidharma said "So you're enlightened already?"

Rabbi David Hartman told me about mind: a man said to a little boy "I'll give you a dollar if you tell me where God is"

— the little boy said "I'll give you two dollars if you tell me where God is not."

Zen is a pair of hands slipped over your eyes from behind and someone saying "Guess Who?" and they wont give in till you start getting mad and then you look and it's someone you've completely forgotten.

Some of the real old Zen Masters of China and Japan were very bright, like the one who rushed around telling everybody "Who dragged this corpse here for you?" (try it and see in the mirror), or the one who fished all day without a line and said he was fishing for the Golden Carp (the fish of truth).

I had a contemporary Zen exchange with Allen Ginsberg, he was sitting in the yard and said "Watermelon," and I say "Why?" as I went into the house for a cup of coffee, when I came out I said "Wouldnt it be awful if students kept asking Zen Masters why?" and he said: "Especially when the Zen Masters dont know why they said it."

Zen is the way you feel when you wake up from a dream about trouble in a far country and you say "Oh boy, good! I dont have to travel all the way back!" And you add, turning over on the pillow, "I didnt have enough money anyway." Where didnt you have enough money anyway — in the dream or someplace? Caw! Caw!

Zen is Peter Orlovsky seeing for the first time a woman in a fur coat thumbing bending over in a trash can for a newspaper, so he leans over to her and says, "Are you sure you're looking for something?"

Zen is like having all your mail forwarded to the Dead Letter Office.

Zen is the madman yelling: "If you wanta tell me that the stars are not words, then stop calling them stars!"

Zen is the moonlit night when I'm walking down the lake and the moon follows me south, and you're walking up the lake and moon follows you north: which one does the True Moon follow?

Zen is Hegel saying "Being and nothing are identical."

Zen is Victor Gioscia driving along seventy miles an hour in his car and I say "Hui-neng said that from the beginning not a thing was" so Victor says "Okay the hell with it! " and takes his hands off the wheel and I yell "No!"

Zen is a man sweeping his walk and raking his leaves.

Zen is the fear of going to work but as soon as you start working everything's forgotten: This haiku by Jōsō describes this and all of Zen as well as anything can:

> Rain begins to fall:
> the roofer turns
> And looks at the sea

Zen is also the promise of mercy as exemplified by the Buddha's left hand being open to Father Sky and the right hand pointing to Mother Earth.

Ten (December 1960)

Ten years ago my good friend Seymour Wyse of London ran his finger across his throat and said: "Jazz killed itself." Couldnt take his word too lightly because as far back as 1941 he'd written an article entitled "Lester Young Is Ten Years Ahead of His Time," in collaboration with myself, and we'd mailed it to Barry Ulanov at *Metronome* magazine never to hear another word again or even get the manuscript back. But I think even Seymour must realize today that jazz is not yet dead. When he left America in 1951 he did add: "But Charlie Parker's trying to do something impossible." I think the first breakthrough since Charlie Parker has been accomplished by Ornette Coleman and Donald Cherry with his little cornet and that it will lead the way, like Parker's way, into a whole new era of jazz. Another sign of a great jazz resurgence is the presence of hundreds of great soloists to implement the new phrase and harmony. Here are only a few names, instrument by instrument, old names and new names, the parade of great wailers who will make the New Wave Jazz pop. Just imagine the list of bassplayers: beginning with the established greats like Percy Heath, Oscar Pettiford, Tommy Potter and Ray Brown we now have a new wave of bassplayers known and unknown like Doug Watkins, Paul Chambers, Sam Jones, Charley Haden (of Ornette's group) (a bassplayer of the future), Eddy Jones, Johnny Orr, Herbie Lewis (young kid), Spanky DeBrest, Wilbur Little, Keeter Betts, George Tucker, Quincy Jones, Mingus and a whole bunch of bassplayers in a softer groove like Dave Bailey, Gary Peacock, Dee Riley, Abdul Malik, Knobby Totah, Leroy Vinegar and Fred Katz who plays cello, and on and on. In the trumpet scene: beginning with Miles, Diz, Donald Byrd and Nat Adderly you go right on to a rejuvenated Clark Terry, sweet Thad Jones, Bill Hardman (who is on the Ornette groove now), Chauncey Adams from St. Louis, Boston Joe Gordon, Richie Williams, Dizzy Reese, marvelous flowing Booker Little, Dupree Bolton (another young kid) and all those sort of West Coast or Soft Groove trumpets like Jack Sheldon, Art Farmer, Tony Fruscella, Jon Eardley, Dicky Mills, Chet Baker (who could have been the greatest and can still be). I mean "softer phrasing."

Of necessity most of this column has to be names. Take the piano scene: the great Thelonious Monk may go down in history as one of the greatest composers who ever lived, in music purely, and he is followed by Horace Silver, Bud Powell (recently waking up in Paris) and Lennie Tristano who has been hibernating and may soon burst out with a bomb of "new piano. " Behind these giants a whole bunch of newcomers are playing with that heartbreaking *grope* that jazz-lovers love: Junior Mantz, Tommy Flanagan, Duke Pearson, Barry Harris, and that swinging beautiful Russ Freeman: and look at the names: Buddy Montgomery, Walter Bishop, Elmo Hope, Horace Parlan, Winton Kelly, Freddy Redd, Red Garland (a strange thinker actually), Richie Hyams, Don Friedman, Ray Bryant, and on and on to endless vistas of piano: Walter Davis Jr., Mal Waldron, John Lewis of the MJQ, McCoy Tyner, Jimmy Jones and others I can't think of and the new "swaying jazz" or "funk" type of pianists like Les McCann and Bobby Timmons. To back them up (I forgot Randy Weston) you have an array of fabulous drummers beginning of course with Art Blakey and Philly Joe and Max Roach probably the greatest but just consider powerful Elvin Jones, Lex Humphries, Roy Brook, Billy Higgins (original thinker), old Kenny Clarke as great as ever, Shadow Wilson, Ocie Johnson, Connie Kaye, Louis Hayes, Chico Hamilton, Rufus Jones and new drummers like Frank Butler and Albert Heath and Al Hairwood. Roy Haynes and Shelly Manne can never change. The guitar players are making fine solos: Kenny Burrell, Wes Montgomery, Billy Bean, Carson Smith, Johnny Smith; and old Billy Bauer is still dreaming over his strings. The alto players are phrasing faster and better than ever: Ornette Coleman can play exactly like Bird if he wants to but he's forged ahead to a new vision: Cannonball Adderly is still growing: behind them fine new altos like Sonny Redd of Detroit, John Handy III, Jack McLean, Charlie Mariano and Al Macusik; and I'm forgetting others and many more than Lou Donaldson, Lee Konitz (who inspired me in 1951 "to write the way he plays"), the magnificent G. G. Gryce, and of course Art Pepper, Bud Shank and any of those tenormen like Zoot Sims or Sonny Stitt who can pick up an alto and make it just as good. Tenor is my favorite instrument and the tenormen today have never been better: starting with John Coltrane, I'd say, a veritable "saint" of music who I understand spends day in and day out playing for himself or in public; and the magnificent "return" of Sonny Stitt who was a buddy of Bird's and apparently went into silence for awhile (listen to him on "Nevertheless," it'll break your heart); and Sonny Rollins, the overpowering John Griffin, Hank Mobley, and one tenorman I think tremendously underrated: Frank Foster. The great new tenor star: JUNIOR COOK. And Harold Land, Benny Golson (all talent), Charlie Rause, Frank West, George Coleman, Jimmy Heath and in that other softer groove I mentioned before: Stan the Man Getz, Zoot Sims, Phil Urso, Brew Moore, Ted Robinson, Jimmy Giuffre, Carmen Leggio and a tenorman I used to like very much who called himself "George Jones." Two of the greatest cornet players who ever lived, on a par with Bix and Hackett, are playing today: Donald Cherry and Don Joseph. Anybody who never heard Lester Young on clarinet might be satisfied with Tony Scott and Buddy DeFranco. They said there would never be blues singers to match Joe Turner and Jimmy Rushing but we suddenly exploded with Joe Williams and Ray Charles and not to mention Sonny Terry on blues harmonica. Great scat singers make old scat look sick, unfortunately: Johnny Hendricks, Babs, and the King, King Pleasure. Pepper Adams I think leads the way in baritone, the field that used to belong to Mulligan, Leo Parker and Cecil Payne. The "New Wave" big bands may yet come: I like Bill Bregman's big studio band, Gil Evans, Les Brown and of course Count Basie, and the new Duke Ellington band is blasting again (viz. "Hey Little Girl"). On trombone you've got Curtis Fuller who phrases so fast and well, Pee Wee Moore, J. J., Kai, Jimmy Nepper and Jimmy Cleveland. Even the flutists wail: Jerome Richardson, Paul Horne, Herbie Mann, and there's an accordion player called Leon Sash who reminds me of what we should have expected from accordion long ago.

So I see Seymour sitting deep in a low easy chair in England as the old sun creeps along the London rooftops, listening to his American LP albums of the new jazz, not moving, listening, listening, realizing jazz isnt dead at all. Hey Seymour!

Eleven (April 1960)

The MAD ROAD, lonely, leading around the bend into the openings of space towards the horizon Wasatch snows promised us in the vision of the West, spine heights at the world's end, coast of blue Pacific starry night — nobone half-banana moons sloping in the tangled night sky, the torments of great formations in mist, the huddled invisible insect in the car racing onwards, illuminate. — The raw cut, the drag, the butte, the star, the draw, the sunflower in the grass — orangebutted west lands of Arcadia, forlorn sands of the isolate earth, dewy exposures to infinity in black space, home of the rattlesnake and the gopher . . . the level of the world, low and flat: the charging restless mute unvoiced road keening in a seizure of tarpaulin power into the route, fabulous plots of landowners in green unexpecteds, ditches by the side of the road, as I look from here to Elko along the level of this pin parallel to telephone poles I can see a bug playing in the hot sun — swush, hitch yourself a ride beyond the fastest freight train, beat the smoke, find the thighs, spend the shiney, throw the shroud, kiss the morning star in the morning glass — madroad driving men ahead. Pencil traceries of our faintest wish in the travel of the horizon merged, nosey cloud obfusks in a drabble of speechless distance, the black sheep clouds cling a parallel above the streams of C B Q — serried Little Missouri rocks haunt the badlands, harsh dry brown fields roll in the moonlight with a shiney cow's ass, telephone poles toothpick time, "dotting immensity" the crazed voyageur of the lone automobile presses forth his eager insignificance in noseplates and licenses into the vast promise of life . . . the choice of tragic wives, moons. Drain your basins in old Ohio and the Indian and the Illini plains, bring your big muddy rivers through Kansas and the mud-lands, yellowstone in the frozen North, punch lake holes in Florida and L. A., raise your cities in the white plain, cast your mountains up, bedawze the west, bedight the west with brave hedgerow cliffs rising to Promethean heights and fame — plant your prisons in the basin of the Utah moon — nudge Canadian groping lands that end in arctic bays, purl your Mexican ribneck, America. Cody's going home, going home.

. . . Home to California eventually where with wife on newhoneymooning Market Street sidewalks of romantic boy-girl Frisco I see the two of them cutting along like ads for the future — bright, neat, Cody his hair ruffled in the wind and over his forehead, a T shirt, clean as snow now, inside a tweed cheap suity sports coat, trousers pressed, rippling and folding in the walk sun, his shoes amazing by the sad gray sidewalk, his hands holding hers, his arms folded, half grinning, an Irish youth almost pretty and certainly handsome and boyish, and her a regular doll of course with blonde upfluffed braids of gold hair and chic suit and high heels and handbag (a suede jacket, by God, with a suede cord belt), tweed and casual cor-duroy herringboning down the aftercloth — It's Cody in the first days of his reformed marriage. He's an institution by himself. He has the strength of the bourgeois and the lumpenproletariat all at once, he Out Marxes Marx, he's a lad. . . His children will look at the snapshot of this vision and say "My daddy was a strapping young man in 1950, he strutted down the street as cute as can be and for all a few troubles he had that Irish fortitude and strength — ah coffin! eatest thou old strength for thy meal, and throw worms?"

How can the tragic children tell what it is their fathers

killed, enjoyed and what joyed in and killed them to make
them crop open like vegetable windfalls in a bin . . . poor
manure, man.

"How could he then — and as they say, after a gruelling
series of voyages overland in old cars and with — and the
nights, fights, tears, reconciliations, packing, sewing up, in
fact all the marriages — so there he smiles in his youth, my
father, my Cody — and now what fodder, what box thing . . ."
Te Deum, the children will imagine gods for their fathers
and myths for the forgotten mistakes of anonymity by glooms
— no hope whatever of gleaning the secret from our ancestral
he-doers and she-makers. He doeth, she maketh it: in the
corn they sing. Blest be the Lord, the Meek, the Union of
these two souls amen. Let us pray in the great dark rains of a
carnage . . . ask for knowledge . . . find a backrest for our
doubt.

"*Tutta tua vision fa manifesta, e lascia pur grattar.*" These
lines are the foundations of a great design.

The First Word

My position in the current American literary scene is simply that I got sick and tired of the conventional English sentence which seemed to me so ironbound in its rules, so inadmissible with reference to the actual format of my mind as I had learned to probe it in the modern spirit of Freud and Jung, that I couldn't express myself through that form any more. How many sentences do you see in current novels that say, "The snow was on the ground, and it was difficult for the car to climb the hill"? By the childish device of taking what was originally two short sentences, and sticking in a comma with an "and," these great contemporary prose "craftsmen" think they have labored out a sentence. As far as I can see, it is two short sets of picturization belonging to a much longer sentence the total picturization of which would finally say something we never heard before if the writer dared to utter it out.

Shame seems to be the key to repression in writing as well as in psychological malady. If you don't stick to what you first thought, and to the words the thought brought, what's the sense of bothering with it anyway, what's the sense of foisting your little lies on others, or, that is, hiding your little truths from others? What I find to be really "stupefying in its unreadability" is this laborious and dreary lying called craft and revision by writers, and certainly recognized by the sharpest psychologists as sheer blockage of the mental spontaneous process known 2,500 years ago as "The Seven Streams of Swiftness."

In the *Surangama Sutra*, Gotama Buddha says, "If you are now desirous of more perfectly understanding Supreme Enlightenment, you must learn to answer questions spontaneously with no recourse to discriminative thinking. For the

Tathagatas (the Passers-Through) in the ten quarters of the universes, because of the straight-forwardness of their minds and the spontaneity of their mentations, have ever remained, from beginningless time to endless time, of one pure Suchness with the enlightening nature of pure Mind Essence."

Which is pretty strange old news. You can also find pretty much the same thing in Mark 13:11. "Take no thought beforehand what ye shall speak, neither do ye premeditate: but whatsoever shall be given you in that hour, that speak ye: for it is not ye that speak, but the Holy Ghost." Mozart and Blake often felt they weren't pushing their own pens, 'twas the "Muse" singing and pushing.

But I would also like to compare spontaneous composition of prose and verse to the incomparable, heartbreaking discipline of the fire ordeal. You had to get through the fire "to prove your innocence" or just die in it "guilty" — there was certainly no chance to stop and think it over, to chew on the end of your pencil and erase something. O maybe you could pause a second or two for another direction but the trick was to act now (or speak now, as in writing) or forever hold your tongue.

In another sense spontaneous, or ad lib, artistic writing imitates as best it can the flow of the mind as it moves in its spacetime continuum, in this sense it may really be called Space Age Prose someday because when astronauts are flowing through space and time they too have no chance to stop and reconsider and go back. It may be they won't be reading anything else but spontaneous writing when they do get out there, the science of the language to fit their science of movement.

But I'd gone so far to the edges of language where the babble of the subconscious begins, because words "come from the Holy Ghost" first in the form of a babble which suddenly by its sound indicates the word truly intended (in describing the story sea in *Desolation Angels* I heard the sound "Peligroso" for "Peligroso Roar" without knowing what it meant, wrote it down involuntarily, later found out it means "dangerous" in Spanish — I began to rely too much on babble in my nervous race away from cantish cliches, chased the proton too close with my microscope, ended up ravingly enslaved to sounds, became unclear and dull as in my ultimate lit'ry experiment *Old Angel Midnight* (*Evergreen Review* and *Lui* in Paris in French). There's a delicate balancing point between bombast and babble.

And now my hand doesn't move as fast as it used to, and so many critics have laughed at me for those 16 originally-styled volumes of mine published in 16 languages in 42 countries, never for one moment calling me "sensitive" or artistically dignified but an unlettered literary hoodlum with diarrhea of the mouth, I'm having to retreat closer back to the bombast (empty abstraction) of this world and make my meaning plainer, i.e., dimmer, but the Space Age of the future won't bother with my "later" works if any, or with any of these millions of other things written today that sound alike.

To break through the barrier of language with WORDS, you have to be in orbit around your mind, and I may go up again if I regain my strength. It may sound vain but I've been wrestling with this angelic problem with at least as much discipline as Jacob.

The little kid in the Lowell House at Harvard, whose professor I was for an hour, looked me right in the eye and asked, "Why do you have no discipline?" I said, "Is that the way to talk to your professor? Try it if you can. If you can you'll pull the rug out from everybody."

My Cat Tyke

There's my cat Tyke, sitting in the Autumn grass eyes slitted to the gold, calm, nothing can bother him not even distant yarps of dogs or boom of upstairs jetliners spreading back four streamers in the singed blue void — Planes for Paris and Bombay, Port Swettenham and Cadiz, & could a cat care? unless Spain cat was brought to sit before him from Madrid? in which case he would chase him out of the yard because ever since I bought the little 4-room cottage for my mother he has been very jealous of interlopers, cats & dogs both, though he lets the birds (even gray mourning doves) eat at their pleasure the breadcrumbs my good mother puts out every morning neatly sliced into dices of bread (also birdseed from the store) — Tyke has a fence keeping dogs out but when cats sneak in he chases them, altho one particular gray male had followed him somehow or smelled his secret entrance thru the tiny cellar window where my mother'd jerrybuilt a rickety old shack cover looking like a Tarahumare shelter outside the dumps of Juarez — Through this shack Tyke could slip into the cellar, by jumping down on a cellar table with two crates on it for steps, pad softly upstairs & shove in the kitchen door (never hooked) to come ma- -wowing to his delicious catfood & milk — This gray cat had learned the trick & one night there was a big screaming fight in the kitchen — Even so the gray cat still comes quietly nosing the kitchen door in & peeks with green eyes to see if everyone asleep & Master Tyke gone a-whoring, in which case he slurps everything up & retreats out the same way —

But these problems of Tyke's I sigh to think are so much purer than mine — I'm standing there all packed & dressed to go take a jetliner to Hollywood to appear on the Steve

Allen TV show over a nationwide network, to read six minutes of my shameful poesy & prose — Does Tyke gulp because millions will be staring at his face Monday night & thinking all kinds of thoughts angry & otherwise about him which can never be better in any case than no thoughts at all, for Tyke is like that Chinese Tao Sage who keeps as low as the valley can be, imitates water in a stream bed, & therefore conquers the valley because he never can be seen upraised anywhere for the purpose of cutting down: the Secret King of the Valley —

So there he is, my sweet cat & brother Tyke, a half Persian Florida alley cat, meditating quietly on his paws, whole body hunched like a Buddha-cat, eyes mostly closed, unwilling to be disturbed by anything, by my goodbye call or roar of overhead jet, just sitting in his November straw sun with the Wisdom of Holy Egypt in all his supple muscles — "And does he jet to the Coast?" I think. "Does he sign contracts, pay taxes, rip open envelopes or grieve in the general horror? No, he stares at the horizon where space disappears into the void within himself and within all things — it's Wednesday & his cat girl is believing at her other end of the neighborhood knowing he'll come tonight — he knows he'll eat his mouse & his mouse eat him — he is hopelessly dejected in eternity; cocksure trapped, yet he couldnt care less ha ha! And at dawn tomorrow when I'll have had my silly self carried 3,000 miles away for ultimate nothingness he'll be hurrying home with his tail down, and:

> Breakfast done,
>   the tomcat curls up
> On the dawn couch

and that's as clear's your nose in the noonday mirror, boy."

The great English poet Christopher Smart said of his own cat: "For I will consider my Cat Jeoffry . . . For he will not do destruction, if he is well-fed, neither will he spit without provocation . . . For every house is incompleat without him & a blessing is lacking in the spirit . . . For he knows that God is his Saviour . . . For there is nothing sweeter than his peace when at rest."

"What Am I Thinking About?"

[In 1969 the editor of the *Chicago Tribune Magazine* asked Jack Kerouac these questions: "What does the author of *On the Road* and *The Subterraneans* think of the hippie, the dropout, the war protester, the alienated radical? Does he have anything in common with them? Does he disown them? Does he qualify as an intellectual forebear of any sort? What is Jack Kerouac thinking about these days?"]

What am I thinking about? I'm trying to figure out where I am between the established politicians and the radicals, between cops and hoods, tax collectors and vandals.

I'm not a Tax-Free, not a Hippie-Yippie — I must be a Bippie-in-the-Middle.

No, I'd better go around tell everybody, or let others convince me, that I'm the great white father and intellectual forebear who spawned a deluge of alienated radicals, war protesters, dropouts, hippies and even "beats," and thereby I can make some money maybe and a "new Now-image" for myself (and God forbid I dare call myself the intellectual forebear of modern spontaneous prose), but I've got to figure out first how I could possibly spawn Jerry Rubin, Mitchell Goodman, Abbie Hoffman, Allen Ginsberg and other warm human beings from the ghettos who say they suffered no less than the Puerto Ricans in their *barrios* and the blacks in their Big and Little Harlems, and all because I wrote a matter-of-fact account of a true adventure on the road (hardly an agitational propaganda account) featuring an ex-cowhand and an ex-footballer driving across the continent north, northwest, midwest and southland looking for lost fathers, odd jobs, good times, and girls and winding up on the railroad. Yup, I'd better convince myself that these thinkers were not on an entirely different road.

But now, where will I turn? O, I know, I'll go to the "top echelons" of American Society, all sleeked up, and try to forget the ships' crews of World War II who grew beards and long haircuts till a mission was finished, or the "dissheveled aspect" of G.I. Joe in the foxholes, yair, the "slovenly appearance" of men and women in 1930s breadlines, and understand that appearance *does* make the man, just like clothes, and go rushing to a Politico fund-raising dinner. House Appropriations Chairman, assistants, Health Directors, Commission Chairman, assistants, Assistants to the Director of Regional Planning, Neighborhood Center Directors, Executive Presidents of Banks, Chairmen of Interior Subcommittees, Officials of the Department of Rehabilitative Services, Planners of the Preliminary Regional Plan, ethical Members of Rules Committees, House Insurance Committees, Utilities Commission entrepreneurs, Expressway Authority Directors, county news hacks, spokesmen, pleaders, applauders, aides and wives in organdy, $2500 worth of food and $5000 worth of booze and the caterer's cut thrown in, for one "lunch," tax-exempt, televised for a 15-second spot in the evening news to show how well they can put on the dog. At your expense.

Here every handshake, every smile, every gibberous applause is shiny hypocrisy, is political lust and concupiscence, a ninny's bray of melody backed by a ghastly neurological drone of money-grub accompanied by the anvil chorus of garbage can covers being banged over half-eaten filet mignons which don't even get to the dogs, let alone hungry children of the absent "constituency."

I'll try to forget that the Hippie Flower Children out in the park with their peanut butter sandwiches and their live-and-let-live philosophy nevertheless are not too proud of being robbed of their simplified attempt at primitive dignity, but the banquet guests are proud, proud. The banquet guests, the Politicos and their grinnish entourage in glistering suits and dresses, paper-shufflers all, plutocrats *salient* with hind paws and forepaws together, last night's *nouveau riche*, would be even prouder if they could get the "non-productive parasite Hippies" to get to work digging new roads and cooking and washing dishes at these fund-raising galas so the dirty punks could at least make cash contributions, or, at best, pay taxes to enable the paper-shufflers to order more paper and copying machines with which they now *rampant* could form a further "planning" committee (of three-year duration, on pollution, sex, think of anything dirty) while sitting back and admiring the view of their back lawn where all the trees that only God can make have been cut down along with the birds' nests.

No, I think I'll go back to the alienated radicals who are quite understandably alienated, nay disgusted, by this scene, but I'll have to try to overlook the fact that the "alienated" radicals and activist Yippies and SDS'ers who pretended holily inside the Hippie Flower movement of a few years ago till their colors withdrew into the basal portions of the chromotophores like the dwarf lizard's have no better plan to offer the grief-stricken American citizenry but fund-raising dinners of their own, and if not for the same reasons, I'd better forget I'd be willing to bet for *worse* reasons.

Because So What if these brand new alienated radical chillun of Kropotkin and Bakunin don't believe in Western-style capitalism, private property, simple privacy even of individuals or families, for instance, or in Jesus or any cluster of reasons for honesty; or in education of course, that is, the bigotry of classic historical scholarship which enables one to know one, the better to see what other ambitious vandals and liars did before; or don't believe in government wrenched away by any others but themselves? Ah, so what if they don't even believe in the written word which is the only way to keep the record straight?

Really, so *What's New* if they would like to see to it that under Timothy Leary's guiding proselytization no one in America could address a simple envelope or keep a household budget or a checkbook balanced or for that matter legible? In fact wouldn't it be better if nobody at all could count change any more and of course forget how to read any kind of book, newspaper or document, the P.O.B.'s (The Print-Oriented-Bastards!) and stick to the psychedelic multimedia nude "Commune" dance at retardate happenings inside of giant plastic balloons, the better to cart the *branle-cul* fools off to camps when used? (Documented as insane, or course.)

In fact, who cares, shucks, Toronto, that if Marshall McLuhan had wanted to be the biggest barbarianizing influence in the globe he couldn't have come up with a better idea (even if you can't go to the toilet nowadays without having an affidavit on it) than that linear reasonableness of the printed word is out, and the jiggling behinds in back of placards are in? (Electronic All-Now mosaic dots on said behinds somewhat suspect.)

Of course the alienated radicals, the would-be fund raisers of the Peking-oriented Castro-jacketed New Left who hate be-necktied plutocrats so much because clothes don't make the man, themselves won't take LSD or STP acid (which stupefy the mind and hand for weeks on end) but will keep perfect records of their own, even incorporate tax-exempt Libertarian Foundations for vocal poets who are really agitational propagandists, why, the alienated radicals, they'll be exuding transactions maybe with the help of a relative who's a lawyer. Their anarchism extends just so far, after all. The relative wants to be a commissar, too, hey. No sense starting trouble unless you get a "top job" straightening it out. Commissar of Chaos, say.

So who care anyhow that if it hadn't been for western-style capitalism so-called (nothing to do with the black market capitalism in Jeeps and rice in Asia), or *laissez-faire*, free economic byplay, movement north, south, east, and west, haggling, pricing, and the political balance of power carved into the U.S. Constitution and active thus far in the history of our government, and my perfectly recorded and legitimatized U.S. Coast Guard papers, just as one instance of arch (non-anarchic) credibility in our provable system, I wouldn't have been able or allowed to hitchhike half broke thru 47 states of this Union and see the scene with my own eyes, unmolested? Who cares, Walt Whitman?

Because the alienated radicals prefer Mao's Peking-style of hitchhiking, "the Maoist dream" where the ideal human being is sent hiking from his intellectual pursuits, the industrial worker from his pad-with-kitchenette, and the wanderer from his pack, to become a "poor peasant." This cultural revolution is called "a war on the Bourgeois and revisionist spirit." To basic Marxism in early sovietist terms this means *partiinost*, complete and eternal rightness of the party cranking machine, and *grazhdanstvennost*, a kind of Everybody-Think-Alike classroom, and *ideiinost*, steel-eyed loyalty to the party and to Everybody-Think-Alike no matter who gets hurt. Addresses anyone? Red China's international propaganda and subversive apparatus is the *Teh Wu* (Do-Thus) section of Peking's over-all *Hai-Wai-Tiaco-Cha-Pu* espionage organization. Russia — the Kremlin's KGB (State Security Committee) at 19 Stanislavakaya street opposite the East German embassy in Moscow. Viet Cong — propaganda headquarters near Ho Chi Minh's French mansion in the center of Hanoi. This leaves everybody "poor peasants" except the bastard Party cadres who figured it all out, even if they have to compromise a little with the "Bourgeois" now, altho I wish I could tell them that the only Bourgeois I ever knew was Paul Bourgeois, a rough-and-tumble French-Canadian Indian high steel worker on bridges who would tell them to go jump in the Lake of St. Louis de Ha Ha.

O, New World! — Yay, if joy were proponent of coin, what grand economy. It's much like: what do you think a parasite is thinking when he's sucking on the belly of a whale or the back of a shark? — "Where did this big, stupid brute get all that blood, not being a parasite like me? How come he's so strong and free, not knowing how to live like I do?" So with human parasites feeding on their juicy national, personal, political, or racial host.

The principles that built our very rocking chair "Rest Your Head," that renaissance straight-line, that linear, rational, yet sentimental care that keeps the heart set on conserving rather than destroying, are what anarchists, who are thieves of the mind, want, just as thieves, who are anarchists of the mind, want the rocking chair.

But now, I'll have to switch and become a "war protestor" and stick to my guns and try to insult the Military-Industrial Complex for safeguarding our offensive weapons inside of an electric armory instead of leaving them out in the rain. I'll try to forget old armory raids. Maybe Jerome Weisner of MIT already does. At least I can always yell "ABM system too expensive!" but who'm I going to blame, Military Industrial Complex? or Industrial Military Complex? or Industrial Civilian Military Labor Academic Complex? or . . . or maybe, yippee! no national right at all to be granted to the United States to defend itself against its own perimeter of enemies in its own bigger scale, that's best. Advised by the pacifists who faced Genghiz Khan. By international pacifist demonstrators who now face further demonstrations by Chairman Mao's IBM warheads.

Or I can always try to see aggression by the U.S. in Viet Nam as different from other armies' "defensive ripostes" and "counter-foils" and the good old *brisk reply* to "blind hatred" — a "lesson" not an attack. I'll try to see the difference between bombing of "civilians" in one town and bombing of "women and children" in another, and "reprisals" instead of raids, and, elsewhere on our map, rocket "warnings" on the very ricepot rooftops of Saigon and Hue by the Viet Cong and brutal United States Imperialist bombings of Ho Chi Minh trail and rails 'round Hanoi. Then I'll get a Ph.D. in the distinguishing of this ideological difference, become expert, disinterested, warm, the diploma being mailed to me by Gen. David Dellinger in Hanoi as a sign I should be grateful and I've done my duty and the word is out I need never be ashamed of myself again, because I'm one of the "kids" who's been out there just like them "doughboys in the trenches Over There," like "our boys in the war effort," yes, "one of the kids down there in the Park" in Chicago 1968 as seen from a quiet third-floor suite by martini-mitted Protest Leaders who look pretty shipshape and pretty presentable as generals go (altho I still think I look silly with that billyclub sticking out of my ear which is also smeared with a bag of you-know-what).

Warm human beings everywhere. In Flanders Field they're piled 10 high.

The Mekong, it's just a long, soft river.

I'll do this, I'll do that —

You can't fight City Hall, it keeps changing its name —

Ah pooey on 'em — you pays your taxes and you passes to your grave, why study their "matters"? Let them present their problematical matters before the zoning board, or present complaint SIX on matters before the kidnapped Dean (problem planning committees for planning problem solutions) 'cause "I've got," as Neal Cassady said, "my own lil old bangtail mind."

I think I'll drop out — Great American tradition — Dan'l Boone, U.S. Grant, Mark Twain — I think I'll go to sleep and suddenly in my deepest inadequacy nightmares wake up haunted and see everyone in the world as unconsolable orphans yelling and screaming on every side to make arrangements for making a living yet all bespattered and gloomed-up in the nightsoil of poor body and soul all present and accounted for as some kind of sneakish, crafty gift, and all so *lonered*. Martin Heidegger says *"Why are there existing essential things, instead of nothing?"* Founder of Existentialism, never mind your Sartre, and also said: "And there is no philosophy without this doozie as a starter." Ever look closely at *anybody* and see that particularized patience all their own, eyes hid, waiting with lips sewn down for time to pass, for something to lift them up, for their yesterday's daily perseverance to succeed, for the long night of life to take them in its arms and say: "Ah, Cherubim, this silly stupid business . . . What *is* it, existence. A lifelong struggle to avoid disaster. Idiot PTA's and Gurus call it Cre-a-tive? Politics, gambling, hard work, drinking, patriotism, protest, pooh-poohings, all therapeutic shifts against the black void. To make you forget it really isn't there, nor you anywhere. "It's like saying, if there are no elephants in the room, then you can safely say the room is empty of elephants. Ah, your immemorial golden ashes shall seem to be scattered anywhere in Paradise."

All caught in the middle.

Ah! I know what I'll do, I'll be like Andy Capp the British comic strip character and go to the rub-a-dub-dub for a bout-a-doubt (Cockney lingo for "pub" and "stout"). After all, doubt parades a lout. And I'll yell "WHAT I NEED IS LESS PEOPLE TELLIN' ME WHAT I NEED!" (©1969 by Smythe.)

So I'll be "generous with the liberality of poets which is conservative to the bone." (©1969 by Donald Phelps.)

"No cede malis" (cede not to malfortune) (don't give into bad times). (©130 A.D. by Juvenal.)

Some deluge.

cityCityCITY

Boys pushing through the combination inter-group deactivator, for juvenile delinquent kicks, and sometimes just young children when they tried to shove through to their ball, had brought up before Congress the subject of laxity of Deactivation. "It's a grave peril to our freedoms," said a spokesman close to sources in Master Center Love (MCL). "It shows a disrespect for ancient tradition in cityCity*CITY* that was accepted without cavil by the older generation. A great many lives of our children, too, are endangered, when their non-deactivated rubber balls fall into a No-Zone and the game of 'push-me-in' takes place, where boys line up behind the brave volunteer and forcibly shove him through the air barrier of the deadly No-Zone where he struggles, choking and turning blue and causing irreparable damage to his lungs, until the ball usually is handed to him by a No-Zone child, as a courtesy, and then ensues the even deadlier game of pulling him back with the pushed-in hand of the leader of the file in Zone, which sometimes fails and results in the death of the child trapped to choke in No-Zone. These practices, plus the delinquent practice of running and throwing oneself against the No-Zone air barrier, which is called Sexing, must be dealt with at the root of their cause; mere punitive punishment, increase of electrocutions, alone, serves no real preventative courtesy to the ideals of Master Center Love and all it has stood for since the Twenty-Eighth Century and the blood shed so willingly before the year One."

This was on the Brow Multivision set, just a little rubber disc adhering to the brow, turned on and off at the breast control; the sensation to a newcomer was of seeing, hearing, smelling, tasting, feeling and thinking the sensation of the vision, which was being waved out of Master Center Love Multivision Studios. M-80, of Zone Block 38383939383-338373 (a number most difficult to refer to, without a Multigraph), (but referred to and duly recorded and Destinated in Master Center Love), walked down the street in the early morning sunshine. M-80 was a kid of thirteen. He had pushed the Multivision down from where he usually kept it on the back of his ear, listened a minute, to the speech about juvenile delinquents, and now was about to slide it back, when the commercial came on and he felt a delicious wave of ecstasy from some spiel about a new Drug . . . "They were saying I couldnt be happy, couldnt be high in the cloudless sky, glad, raving to joy, but no, say, hear me, I went and got myself a tube of 17-JX, *we* call it Jex, and I took out two tablets, and swallowed with water, and instantly, almost at once! there stole over me the incomparable ecstasy of a REALLY free and at the same time POLITE compound. I said to myself 'These MCL chemists who prepare this Drug for the people of cityCityCITY show that they really know the meaning of LOVE: they have gone all out to provide myriallions and myriallions with the Best, the Most Polite, Courteous, Loving that ingenuity can devise and Merits buy . . !" But M-80 wasn't listening to the announcer; he was busy enjoying the four or five seconds of bliss allowed by the commercial, as a teaser. People all over cityCityCITY were putting in calls this minute to the Super Drugway; soon you'd see them flying around, to their destination; "nobody'll even be on the street," sneered the boy, who wanted to play. "U-21'll stay home and try his old Drug, and H-30'll sleep on it . . . Golly! Atheism! There's a pool of water — a real pool of water!" His heart thumped. He had never seen a pool of water in his life, except in Multivision in their history shows, showing how, in the days before rain was diverted from cityCityCITY, moisture used to fall from the skies and form in the streets and blocks of old cities. "There's been a leak!" thought the kid frantically. "What'll they say? Wow!" He rushed up to the pool. Marvelously it reflected the blue perfect sky, with a little ripple only. It was a clean puddle, just a little dust on the edges. He touched it wonderingly, squatted. It was only 8 in the morning and he was the only one who'd seen it. He ran his finger around, stepped in. "It's just like when they electrocute a block and forget to sweep out a dead man ash. Golly zoo Athies! Romanticism! This is going to kill dad." He ran to his house, singing happily some gurgled crazy kidyell of happiness. "Ha, ha, ha," he crashed into the house, interrupting his father, T-3 at breakfast. "What's it, kid?" — wiping his mouth. "A pool of water? Who ever heard of such a thing? Lemme see." They went out together, their crepe-foam shoes sliding softly over the steel-plate street with its bolts at intervals like shiny knobs. The pool lay in a depression formed by an old accident, when an insane old man had thrown the Computer of Merit out of the front window and put a dent in the street. "Hmm," said T-3, Prime Minister of Block 38383939383-338373, a tall handsome man with thick temple gray and a bushy head of hair still jet black in parts, frowning thickly now, "it looks like somethin went wrong somewhere. Couldnt be the Raindar, the Umbrella Command never had any trouble with electronics that I know of, tho there's a theory among some of the MCL wiseguys, about infiltration of Activation agents in the Command . . . a joke on somebody. Let's see . . . a leak in the next plate? But the water wouldn't get through from the No-Zone. What the divine hell could it be? Aw well, it's a puzzle. I'll bring it up with the girls. Son, the day women took over all the central organization of world government, wow, lookout, that was it . . . The day my grandfather envisioned, he told me too, when women get a hold of the whole works and you have to kowtow every morning to a dike martinet, that's your red wagon . . ." T-3 called M-80 "son" but in actuality he was only adopted; all the children of the world, after birth in Central Deactivation, where Deactivator disks were riveted into their breastbones prior to Connection in their given Zone Block, were assigned to various parents, according to the Computer of Infinite Merit in MCL (one of the most, if not THE most complicated mechanical brains ever put together; its central secret feature obtained around a mathematical principle relatively unknown, something to do about the chasing of the Zero to Infinity, a constant process that kept equations spinning dizzily on the Dial, you saw thousands of them flashing on and off, vibrating, sending off waves of computation that you could almost sense sprinting to keep up with the race of the zero and still turn out Estimates of Merit, General and Local, by which the government was run). Some people even went so far as to state that Master Center Love itself was a computation, ever-changing, from the Computer of Infinite Merit, but the truth was, Master Center Love had for centuries emanated from the inner core of the High Women of the world, whose system of succession had never been revealed . . . It was *Political*. M-80 was assigned to his Zone block by the computation of the machine. His real (seminal) parents he would never know, because they were in other Zone Blocks.

The world was the earth; every square inch was covered with electrical steelplate. The ocean had long ago been covered with earth acquired from surrounding planets. cityCityCITY was the world; every square inch of the world steelplate was covered with the Three Types of Levels of cityCityCITY. You saw the skyline, of steel skyscrapers, far away; then beyond that, like a ballooned imitation of the same skyline, rising way beyond and over it, vastly larger, the second level of cityCityCITY, the City level; beyond that, CITY, like a dim cloud, rose huge on the horizon a vast phantasmal skyline so far away you could barely see it, yet it rose far above the other two and far beyond. Those three levels were to facilitate the ingress of sunlight into the various people-flats. The cityCityCITY Tri-Levels were: one tenement ten miles high; the second, fifty miles; the third, a hundred miles high; so that from Mars for instance, you saw the earth with its complete CITY everywhere looking like a prickly ball in the Void. The prickles represented one vast domicile of millions upon millions upon myrillions. In each Zone Block lived only about 2,500 people; but there were billions of Zone Blocks. M-80 was our hero's name; but it was also the name of billions and myrillions of other boys, each with his zone number. His full name was, thus: M-80 38383939383-338373 . . . Population kept increasing continually. It was necessary at intervals to electrocute entire Zone Blocks and make room for a new group culled from slags and miscalculations in the system. Deactivation which prevented people from leaving their own Zone Blocks, was a necessary caution against the chaos which would have resulted from an over-populated Movement over the crowded steelplate of the world. Migrating to other planets was out of the question; especially after centuries of Self Enforced Deactivation. Other planets in the immediate vicinity of earth had been denuded of life and turned into Deactivator Bases and Laboratories, Deactivating all that part of the universe around the earth. Outside raged the life of the Universe, where Activation reigned. Many were the space ships from unknown planets who'd come crashing against the No-Zone of earth and disintegrated in mid-air; many the meteors met the same fate. Nobody questioned the wisdom of Master Center Love in refusing to have any contact with the rest of the universe. Activated . . . a word written in black letters dripping with red ink . . . ACTIVATED, you'd see it written on superseptic toilet walls of the cityCityCITY, with lewd drawings. It was a word whispered in dark sex rooms, turned into a colloquial dirty-word. "Activate me." For all anybody knew, the rest of the universe was completely hostile as well as Activated; no one was taking any chances. But for centuries there had been a steady infiltration of Activationists, and of Activationism. Congressional Committees had investigated. Traitors were found; at least they seemed to be guilty of Activationist activities. The means were through propaganda via Multivision and via certain subversive drugs with telepathic compounds by which the Activationist was said to telepathize propaganda around Master Center Love . . . One Activationist was believed to be behind one of the famous boners in the history of cityCityCITY. Everybody was lying around one day enjoying the afternoon comedy show, Jexed to the gills ("I'm telling you I was HONORED that afternoon, why I was *so* honored . . .") when somebody at Master Center threw the Panic Switch, which sets off the Warning throughout the world of the impending destruction of the Outer Zone Barrier. (Also it is the switch that transmits directly individually to a single Zone Block ten seconds before it is to be electrocuted.) Using it as a warning of impending destruction of the Outer Zone Barrier naturally has never been known to be needed. Zone Blocks are eliminated at the rate of sixteen a day, but with the world so vastly populated, densely, deeply 100 miles down and 24,000 miles around, it was rare that a Zone Blocker could remember at some time in his life witnessing the doom of his nextblock neighbor on either of the four sides. You could see four other zone blocks but you couldn't put your hand through the No-Zone Air, unless pushed, and at great pains, into it. "Yes I remember seeing the north Zoneblock next door here, burned, in '306 . . . it was awful . . . everybody turned black . . . you saw em come runnin outa the house at the warning and still runnin on the steelplate and then they burn black and crisp up . . . there warnt any smoke much . . . I hope never to see it again."

"You think it'll ever happen to our Zone Block?" (a kid).

Wherein comes the famous saying of the world, "If it does you only got ten seconds to worry about it."

The goof at Master had thrown this switch, but for every Zone Block in the world, so that for a moment, everywhere in the world in the trillions of billions of Zone Blocks up and down and all around the globe people rushed out of their houses screaming, sending a human vibration, they say, into the sky, that was said to have almost destroyed the No-Zone Air Barrier, and was the supposed intention behind the plot. Studies were being made century after century to ascertain the effect of such a vast human vibration on the Electronics Wall (Great E Wall) . . . Nothing had ever been unearthed concerning the mystery of the panic broadcast. But it was Activationist work.

Ideas of Activation had been brought onto the earth-globe via the only form of Activated life in the universe that was capable of penetrating the Great Electronics wall: beings on a level of certain rarity that enabled them to swim, veil-like, pale as ghosts, through the Wall and through the people of earth, yet communicating thoughts and ideas. For a long time they were said to be Tathagatas from a Buddha-land but this was refuted in the year '682 by a great Mechanical Scholar who said: "The incidence of supernormal and superreal existence, or isness, on a level of communication via mental conception, is .0008753 impossible, and therefore, After the Zero, on a basis of .3578 returning from the Void Echo Decimal, of no pathoactive significance." It was established then, that these beings were normal beings in a different vibration, not supernormal beings beyond life. Nothing beyond life had as yet found the light of scientific verification. These Beings, these Activation Agents, were the terrors of the world; the troops of Devils of Gothic times were replaced by these pale phantasmal insinuators from Outside, called Actors. This name was referred philologically back to ancient times when disorderly elements were known as "actors" in early trade unions; it all tied up psychologically; now the "actors" were almost impossible to detect and came from other worlds. It was strange. It was always sunlight because of the Raindar Umbrella that prevented moisture from wetting the dangerous electrical hotplate which was the world. The streets were usually empty. Except in the morning, on Market Days, when Drugs, L-Pumps, Computers of Merit, various gadgets, doodads, delicacy pills, etc. were exchanged at the proper marts. Illicit Actor Fumes were sold in forbidden little jars; Actor Fumes came from the emanation which an Actor left when it passed thru a jar, apparently by intention; the sniff of it had the peculiar effect of inducing a certain blissful feeling that was accompanied by a vitamin lapse, or false recharge, that made it impossible to inject L (Love, the official cityCityCITY drug, used by everyone from birth, by law); with the effect of actor fumes, a man of this world was left wide open for telepathic messages from Actors infesting the air; nothing Multivision could send out could combat this, once the victim had a sniff of Actor Fumes, or Ghost, as it was called; it was so powerful and so sweet to the senses the weaker elements of the population were all addicted; it was easy to get, the Actors saw to that, by merely passing themselves through every jar in the world; jars became illegal. Actors began fuming themselves in people's breastpockets; all an addict had to do was bend down and sniff, but this never had the total effect of a good enclosed jarful; the Breast Sniff became the minor evil of the two. Breastpockets of any kind were abolished. Later, pants pockets; cavities of all kinds in clothing, walls, surfaces. Certain addicts became adept at storing fumes in their mouths; certain sexual defectives found all kinds of new thrills. Juvenile delinquents hung around corners holding their hands cupped, after dark, to catch fumes if any. "Man, I'm zoned."

"What's wrong with Master Center World Drugs, that a little whiff of Actor Fumes, or Ghost as it is known in the street, Jar Bang or Breast Sniff, gets everybody going in the wrong direction? Activationism is behind this; research, unending struggle in our laboratories and computatoriums and Mechanical Universities, in our whole Machine, must be banded together to find a solution to this invasion which may only be the prelude to an unheard-of catastrophic deluge from Otside." They called it "Outside," like 20th Century (Pre One) (PO) jailbirds. "The world is going up in flames!" cried the prophets of doom. "All respect for ancient values is deteriorating. People wander off into the realm of Activated thoughts, influenced by Fumes. Or if not that, outcries are raised against the Computer Administration, complaints that such and such a Zone Block was chosen instead of another . . ."

"Five Zone Blocks in my very district have been electrocuted in the past 156 years counting yesterday's Elimination — yet nothing, NOTHING is being done to ascertain why the Computer Administration has not launched an Investigation into possible administrative defects at Center Love that may have played a role in this needless slaughter of District Seventythree."

"Now wait a minute, you can't tell District President that any kind of indelicacy has been involved. My dear man, let us take an instance, District Seventyfour, right next door, three million people and more, have had to put up with as many as eight Zone Block eliminations in the past 150 years, this means twenty thousand District Seventyfours have had to be Eliminated, Security bless their souls . . .

"No, if the world is to keep up its Security Calm, and panic and dissolution and restlessness are to be dispelled, it's going to have to be a new inner movement in the Master Center Love, radiating NEW vigor via Multivision to the Multitude, NEW ideals of Love, a NEW DEAL in Master Center Love, then your fumes'll fade, then your prophets of doom will say 'We should have known better, this old steelplate that only looks like an old marl spike in the universe, is built on solider ground than the ground of Activation spooks with their head-in-the-clouds attitude towards realities of life.' Overpopulation has always given the people what it wants. There may come a day when Depopulation may come to be necessary at last . . . this is the day when Master Center Love shall have to disappear from the cup of this universe . . . this will be the day for the invasion and the rape of cityCityCITY by Activators from Outside . . . and centuries of human effort, mechanical genius and Love shall have turned to dust of failure . . . Overpopulation, now a Legislation 86 Centuries old, stands behind You, and You, and You, and You, and You, and You, and You, and You, and You, and You, and YOU YOU YOU! Let not Depopulation come to Master Center Love!"

The Computer of Infinite Merit worked out supermathematically not only the amount of hours put in by everybody in the world listening to Multivision Love Broadcasts, but because of its contact with the various multibillion disks upon the breastbones of mankind, by a method of such high mechanical mystery, almost mystical in its farreaching significance and political depth, it computed the intensity of the communicant's attention to Love. These complicated figures were broken down by Data Divisions of the General Computer Command, and it was the sum of these figures that had to do with the Merit accumulated by both the individual of a Zone Block and the whole Zone Block together in common merit.

When a Zone Block was chosen for Electrocution, Elimination from life, it was because of the low Merit Average of the whole 2500-odd community. Home Computers of Merit were in use, by which people could keep track of their own average; but some people just didnt care. The Loveless Brothers didnt care. The Loveless Brothers didnt even bother to tune in their Multivision and would have nothing to do with either general Drugs or L the Love Drug. These were the bums of the community, and usually were seen in the streets, sitting, talking. They had homes, they had their cells like everyone else. They contributed dismal scores to the general average of a Zone Block, and of course they were resented and even persecuted. So shiftless were they, sitting there all day with no place to go because Deactivated at birth, and yet not oriented to life in their Zone Block due to their refusal to imbibe the proper drugs, they became motionless and dreamy. Kids never paid attention to Loveless Brothers, brushed them aside sometimes.

It was dusk. The air was filled as always with the vague, dull odor of burning atomic rubber from the continually flying myriads of guided freight missiles bringing uncounted goods from the Drugway and the "Nutrish" (the Nutrition Commissariat). Shoving a Food Pill down his throat, swigging it down with a dash of synthetic dry water, little M-80 ran out to wait for his father, T-3, hoping for news about the official reaction to the pool of water. M-80 stood there, wrinkling his nostrils because he'd never liked that smell of dry rubber of the Synoids flying around up there, tho after a lifetime of smelling it he couldnt quite detect it either. No one else seemed to mind. "M-80 has got too many ideas in his head." — "He certainly complains a lot." — But M-80, standing there, his hair motionless in the dusk, eyes lowered, wondered if he ever would escape. If there was such a thing.

Even when he saw his father stepping out of the Ministry

Van. The Van was made of steel and was operated by two
armed guards who came each morning, flying in silently (but
always leaving a faint odor of wet ashes in the still air, smoul-
dering, all-pervasive, nauseating to M-80 when he stepped
out for afterbreakfast play). The guards opened the
Dezoning door, the most secretly guarded door of the realm
unless you name the door of Master Center Love the inner
bedroom of the Love Exec. The minister of Zone Block
Number So and So stepped in as ordered, with briefcase, as
contact was made with his breast-disk by the diskfinder in
the guards' hands. Two guards were used to point this diskfinder, to offset the possibility of one guard, without being
resisted, turning the diskfinder on the wrong subject in some
attempt, as there had been many in older times, to effect an
escape from Deactivation into the inner Sanctums of Master
Love from which this one heavily guarded carrier was limit-
edly sent to fetch the ministers of the realm, duly elected.
When the Minister, partially and temporarily Activated and
saved from belly strain by the soothing counter-action of the
diskfinder in the rocket room that takes him there, is ordered
to step out into the steelplate of Master Center Love, their
occurs a reverse process, the diskfinder's taken away.
Deactivation takes on full force again but now a marvelous
new sensation takes place, like walking into heaven. Master
Center Love is neither Deactivated nor Activated, there is no
such arbitrary conception there; as a result, Deactivation
immediately ceases, and the Minister is free to get on with
the day's business with the other Ministers and Districters,
all from a variety of different Zone Blocks and all similarly
brought to work. The formula for the arbitrary conception-
lessness of neither Deactivation nor Activation had been
developed in the machine known as the Brain Halo, which
divined equations, proof of equations, disproofs of equations,
balancing them all together, so skillfully, so complicated, a

thousand wires running into a million larger ones that grew and snaked and vined their way in the tangled Wire Room of the Brain. This formula was put to use in Deactivation Headquarters of Master Center Love and sent through. But everyone remained with his Deactivation disk, immune, till the return to the No-Zone of the general Zone Block world of cityCityCITY. Who in Master Center Love was *not* Deactivated? It was the highest known sacrilege to say that anyone on earth could ever be Activated; that anyone had not been born Deactivated was absurd, ridiculous, lies. "If there's someone there in that Woman Room that aint Deactivated, and goes around traveling to the other universe, and's running OUR universe, then I hang up my tube and lay back and become a Loveless Brother cause brother, that means we're all being played a wood — and I dont mean chemical wood."

You'd hear sometimes on murmurous afternoons speeches among the people emanating from noisy sleepSleepSLEEP Halls, where you went to sleep up the Love, or to talk. "I dont give a gerl dang toot; if Master Sinner Love sends me out to that blue horizone with a shot of electrical ouch in my arse, I'm damn sure I aint gonna believe in em on the way out." etc. "Yesh, call me a Loveless Brother if I dont feel the same damn glassed way, gas me."

"What did they say Pa?" yelled M-80 rushing up as his father stepped from the Ministry Van onto the good old steelplate of 38383939383-338373 . . . (that happened to be the queer number of this particular block, and was noted for its strangeness, and commented upon by old citizens, and looked on as a bad sign: "We'll get it soon for sure!") — His father looked worried: lines showed under his eyes. "I've had a strange day, Em child. Wait, let me gather my thoughts, before we talk, let those guards go. I've never felt so oppressed before . . . it's been a strange day."

" — the water — "

"Precisely, the water, the water has got everyone worried
. . . I don't understand . . . it's something about something
about something I just didnt hear when the door closed . . .
And tomorrow I'll know what it's all about but they just left
me in the dark today . . . Something about a similar incident
at such and such a time, water leaking into a Zone Block,
something about Activation activities, always that of course,"
(aside) "they'll find a reason in their black gowns to give a
name to everything, hell and heaven and both the east and
west of themselves, and have funerals on the sly when the
winds dont bring honor" — "they'll find a god damn name
for our death in this block." — He went in to his wife, and to
supper, and a quick tune-in on Multivision to see if there was
any talk yet, any hints from the more casual commentators,
any mad gloved hand maybe he could find in the program
tonight, always so dull and the same — "Love is Patience,
what is my rush to call it dull!" he reprimanded himself, and
worried . . . He was a man on the verge of a nervous break-
down, but held himself together physically and sometimes
physically he'd feel the straining of his components, about
to fall, break down too; he did 32 pushups every morning;
once he'd wanted to do as many pushups as his age, but
now he was a good old healthy taped-together Drugfed
cityCityCITYite of 198 and that was out of the question.
Nothing on Multivision that he could see; tho for a half hour
he lay dreamily listening to some own thought of his suspi-
cions of some point in a sly remark he imagined he heard
during a commercial, "but a cornmercial, what's the matter
with me, looking for news in the commercial? . . . *but that's
where it is,*" he couldn't help having the eerie afterthought,
full of sinister self-assurance. His hair stood on end. Burn,
burn . . . this was the secret thought of all cityCityCITY . . .
not, as in ancient times, Death, Death, I'll grow old and die,

but now old age and death had been checked, so much so that there was a better chance of death by Block Electrocution than by death from really old age in the 300's (which no one, curiously, wanted, it apparently being too long a time for life of any mentally conscious kind). One eminent Mechanic had said: "The quotient of care-to-live decreases in ratio to age; past the 250 mark the quotient is near nil; at 300 there is no substantiality to the quotient warranting the continuance of a living organism." Famous pessimists had reached very old age and left messages of horror to their Block before, senile and most-asleep in the torpor of 400 and 500's, they went up in smoke with the others on the Shock Day.

Shock Day . . . the name was written as by great dark clouds on the blue horizon, some calendars depicted the imagined scene of Shock Day with the homily in large letters, "Trust in Love to take you there." Or, "Be polite to the forces of your Love." And some Alexandrinisms like "Love, You'll Burn it" were featured as jokes in the salons of intellectuals around MCL Hexagon. The Hexagon housed over 20 million government employees and provided Deactivation free while they were there; when fired, they were thrown back into the humdrum ZoneBlock life. In the Hexagon, L Pumps to facilitate the intake of L from Center via L Drug were also provided for government workers. Everyone had L drug free at birth, by law. It was contained in a steel amulet riveted to the outside of the breast-disk just below the place where the Merit Numbers showed counting like the counters on a speedometer. For instance, T-3's disk had a large T-3-38383939383-338373 engraved and fretted, and right under that, the merit counters, and the amulet containing the life-supply of Love Drug. But with an L pump there was no need to pump in the Love Drug yourself; that was for the working people of the world, the "Pumpers," while, for the more fortunate the L pump just worked it in for you. The general theory that you cant have a world completely populated with unoccupied masses here prevailed, of course, for tho it would have been easy to relieve Pumpers of their all-day duties as self L-pumpers of Love Drug, authorities in Master Center Love, perhaps unrightly influenced by some ancient traditions still adhered to in the heat of change and progress, still held that somewhere in the world there must be *some* physical motion and effort, besides the mechanical motion of the machine, for reasons of courtesy to the forces of "nature," perhaps for reasons of unconscious psychological imitation of the machine now that motion was no longer really necessary — The highest cityCityCITY Love Official could be motionless the livelong day receiving her (the highest officials were woman) L and her Multivision in a quiet room, stay like that for months, years, a whole lifetime, it wasnt necessary to move any more. So the "Pumpers" complained of their bitter lot. You saw their darkened faces snarling in the windless air. Nothing moved but a few slow futile sinister gestures of speakers, generally you'd lie there pumping in your Love looking out the window at the empty afternoon steelplate. Sometimes a Loveless Brother shuffled by, cupping his hands together to catch some Action . . . The air however swarmed with freight missiles gayly rushing to their destinations. The Machine was doing the moving for man and still man wanted less and less to move. "Blimey crackerjacks, but if them rich sonsaguns can sit there all day their lard tail on the couch of foam from midnight to midnight and all the kicks in the book, why can't we?"

"It's because you cant have all the people in the world *rich!*"

"Some's got it and some aint."

"Some crap thru burlap and some fart thru silk I say."

"Here I am pumpin and pumpin all day wasting myself to

the bone while these lazy pale tat cottonpickin mother activators go around getting themselves free-rided thru ecstasy.
Why do *I* have to struggle through and them just loaf!"

"Pumpers and Mumpers aint got no jemumpers!" sang the
kids in a favorite street song. Streets had no sidewalks or
curbs. "Galumpers and galumpers . . ." "And if the rich got
curbs, I got blurbs, in Love Magazine," sang the popular W-
70, the Sleepsinger at the Hall.

In the morning Ministers went to work, flying in the
Ministry Van with the two unfriendly diskfinder guards. It
was the rule never to speak to them, only to answer when
spoken to. This was a precaution taken in Master Center
Love, among many others, to establish a gulf of personality
between Minister and guards, to obviate any chance of
friendship, favor, preference stepping into the picture of
impersonal daily flight to work in the mornings and back to
the home Zone-block at night. No Minister had ever been
able to escape his block, or escape the Ministry Van enroute
to MCL or find his way out of MCL once delivered there to
that marvelous wave of neither Activation or Deactivation
that equalled everything out and made you free — but the
walls were thick. The walls of the Kremlin had never been so
thick, the walls of Jugurtha lesser guarded.

MP's stood around with diskfinders, ready to pull an errant
Minister into a Van with the force of the magneto . . . M-80's
Pop, popularly known as Tee, stepped out of the van and felt
the arbitrary conception fade from his disk and from his
brain. "Here you are, Tee. Heard the latest on your pool of
water?"

"No, what . . ."

"You *havent* heard?"

"No" —

Someone was nudging the speaker, he clammed up, grimly
his lips came together. People were whispering. Ministers

and Districters standing all over the steelplate plazas, smoking Jex, rifling thru their briefcases, arguing, waving . . . it was the customary half hour recess before opening of the day's Session. A ripple of attention seemed to be focusing on Tee this morning, but you couldnt always tell, it seemed to be going in other directions too. At least one of the gathered 9,000 Ministers of the "G" area of cityCityCITY daily received notification of the decision to electrocute his block and himself; you heard sometimes lamentable moans rising from the dignified halls of Congress. "When an electrocution takes place brother you gets flown back by the dim guards now and grim they are by now, and you're stepped out on the steelplate of your block and told to stay there, via diskfinder, and the warning is immediately sounded by the guard, setting off the 10 second panic switch all set to go in the Computer works — you see people running out of the apartments, you see upset pumps of L and Comps of Merit spilled and people crawling on the steel begging for mercy but it lasts only a few seconds, and your last glimpse is of the Minister himself standing there in the airless void smelling of dim burnt rubbery ashes with one hand in his coat lapel, like Napoleon, eyes to heaven, boom, up goes the block in sizzles and crackles of hot smoke, as the guards fly away . . . everyday routine with them . . . to them it's known as Hot Dog Day —

"Ah well, such is Overpopulation," was the popular saying. Taps, some called it.

And this is what happened to our Minister T-3. He was informed and notified that clay. Confirmation. Look out, he ran back to the toilet and threw up and they put the diskfinders on him and dragged him back to the Van, tho he would have willingly walked, straight and unafraid of death, tho inwardly trembling. But once he'd been sick and straightened up in the toilet and even combed his hair and adjusted clothing for a grand finale to his life in front of his cohorts . . . they dragged him, like a hoodlum who hasnt done anything, like a saint who's suddenly afraid to die.

It all began at 9 AM. In the committee room Districter G-92 (Goldie) who'd never liked Tee because Tee had voted against his idea in '754 — *O, where had the love of the people wandered?* — Goldie's bill was to centralize Love further into MCL and not concentrate so much on spreading it among the people, who only wasted it. It was a reactionary move by a reactionary thick-headed usurper of other people's natural rights, plainly. Tee had organized a group of Ministers and even two Districters to prepare opposition to this measure . . . For just a Minister Tee had shown remarkable strength. Goldie was the kind of Districter who should never have been promoted from Minister nor elected among the people of his block in the first place. But with some front he'd put on, carefully cultivated for years, to advertise himself as a tireless champion of some kind, for some Cause, whatever Cause they wanted (tho they never caught him taking his secret nap in the afternoon chair . . . tireless, indeed) , he'd worked his way up high in MCL and was even highly regard-ed by Women in the high Courts . . . ("shows how much real love they must have up there, not pumped in") —

Is there such a thing as real love? was a popular question.

So now Goldie had a look of triumph on his face, and since Districters were always notified before Ministers at Special Sessions, Tee now divined "My block's getting it this morn-ing (I got ten minutes or less to live) and he knows it" — But a motion was started up by Tee's friends, to pass a vote around on an Anti-No Zone Pushing bill, aimed to curb the juvenile delinquents and put a stop to the practice altogether by anyone, punishable by individual electrocution. Tee's friends wanted poor Tee to live at least an extra hour . . . to gather his soul up. "Soul" was a popular superstition. Tee saw clearly the reason for the move and the measure. He saw despicable Goldie, showing his teeth, looking oddly like ancient pictures of the Devil with his long sinuous ears and the curve of his arched brows and the particular demonism in the glitter of his eyes or of the glasses before his eyes or of both in conjunction, something hellish Tee prickled all over to see it.

He suddenly saw snakes swarming all around Goldie, the undulating motion of thousands of Ministers. "Life is a snake. What do I lose when I lose the snake? I lose my writhing properties."

He stood up. Goldie was putting in a counter-measure to make the announcement of Electrocution Elimination at once. This meant Tee had ten minutes to live instead of an hour. The giant loudspeaker thundered: "LOVE."

Everyone hushed. The great Voice of Love came over the microphone. "ZONE BLOCK ANNOUNCEMENTS. PROPOSED AMENDMENTS AND EMENDATIONS OF PROGRAM. MEMBERS OF THE MINISTRY HAVE REQUESTED IMMEDIATELY THE VOTE ON THE ANTI-NO ZONE PUSHING BILL. MEMBERS OF THE DISTRICT REPRESENTATION HAVE IN A SUBSTI-TUTE MOTION TO ANNOUNCE THE BLOCK ELIM-INATIONS AND THEN VOTE. O, LOVE, HERE ARE THE NUMBERS OF THE ZONE. BLOCKS TO BE ELECTROCUTED THIS MORNING AND THEIR MINISTERS NUMBER 3838393938383-338373, MINIS-TER T-3 . . . (Voice pauses for speech).

And the Voice of the Woman droned off and Tee stood still, all the eyes of the men who had tried to help him, show-ing piteously in a general stare towards him, and the eyes of his enemies burning to leer his way. The two Van guards approached at once, unsheathing and turning on their disk-finder, both clutching to special side handles on it, pointing at Tee.

"Farewell sweet friends, sweet fellow students of young and happy days . . ." cried Tee to the assembly — "May the hope of the sun or whatever the sun, or hope, or hopes themselves, multiplied, put together by whatever measurements of light, or of actuality, come to you — either by grace, intention, by self assistance, by courage, will, compassion to live — and you find love, real love, if such a thing there be, if such a world indeed there here be now, if — "

O, LOVE HERE ARE THE NUMBERS OF THE ZONE BLOCKS. NUMBER 8386294853008-290490, MINISTER Y-16 — " boomingly interrupted the Voice of Love, cutting Tee's speech short, because the time allotted for speeeh was ten seconds and no more; many's the doomed Minister in his heat of sadness and eloquence who ran over his time — One distinguished Mechanic had made his estimate: "If Ministers were allowed liberal uninterrupted speech time at the announcement of the Electrocution of their blocks, and assuming that the average length of these speeches would be seven minutes, at the barest minimum, the time comsumed and taken at the expense of the work of Love is calculated at sixteen million four hundred and thirty six thousand five and hundred twelve man-years, which, multiplied to the man-quotient, would have meant the loss of 764,096,264,740,862,398 tats of manpower (.Mp), (minus deduction for electronical loss) (and leak). Therefore the ten second rule is imperative to our Machine."

The diskfinder caught Tee, he was dragged to his plane. He sighed with relief in his struggles as he remembered that he had wisely chosen the night before to arrange the escape of his son. Not a moment could be lost now. The moment he was in the Van, and saw the blurred faces of the Ministers of the whole Hexagon vanish, he tore the skin off his fingertip and set off the telemercurator in the secret homemade rocket ship at home.

Zoom! off went little M-80 with his helmet on, he'd been waiting all day seated at the controls, on orders from his father, wondering what it all meant. Now he understood everything! Soon he could see the earth ball growing smaller and smaller back of his tail jet and then suddenly, after some 30 seconds, the flash of electrocution taking place down there in one of the zones — Zone Block 3838393983-338373 had gone up!

"Pa! Ma!" he cried — No sound. Traveling faster than the speed of sound all he could hear was the great dazzling hush of silence persisting and persisting in his ears with no change, no stress, no frightful anxiousness — "There's a Great Smile behind it all!" he suddenly realized intuitively, not knowing where the idea came from — As he went higher and higher his thoughts grew lighter and more ethereal and finally he had no more thoughts and woke up only after a long time in the pitch darkness of some outer chillicosm, realizing that it had all been like a great sad dream, a vision in the mind — that it was only what it was — "Whether as worlds and cities and universes, or whether as nothingness and emptiness, what difference does it make?

He took out his father's letter that he'd been instructed not to open till the panel showed red altimeter lights: -

"Dear Em, By the time you read this, if you read it, I'll be dead and your mother will be with me. Nobody knows where we're all going. When you were born the attendant at Birth Deactivation omitted to rivet a disk in your breast and you were delivered to me non-deactivated. I realized it was a sign. I made a false disk and put it on you so no one would know, then began careful plans that spanned a decade of personal research and hard work late into the night, and the rocket that has now taken you to safety was built, into which,

I poured all my energies and hopes, the eternities bless you and keep you. It was my life's dream to see that you would get out of this Overpopulated Totalitarian trap. I can only say now that the attendant who omitted to Deactivate you, was *not* an attendant, but some form of awakened ghost, the first of many to come on earth.

If and when your rocket lands on some solid planet where you can spend the rest of your natural days living off the concentrated foods I have stored for you in the rear compartments, think of me as your poor old father who did what he thought best and wishes you happiness whichever unknown form it's liable to come to you now — And pray — pray — for I believe that our reward is without end, we just dont know it, OUR REWARD IS WITHOUT END, and it comes to us in some ghostly afterway that must have something to do with the common essence of all things and has to do with what we were before we thought we were born . . . it'a ONE THING, ONE perfect emptiness of light without end. Bless you and gooobye. Your pop, T-3-38383939383-338373, 3-12-986"

The rocket wobbled on and on, like the lonely sensation of thinking.

Editor's Note

In the editing of this volume I have been greatly aided by the work of Ann Charters in her Bibliography and by Marshall Clements in collection of the texts. I also owe debts of gratitude to Barry Gifford and to John Sampas.

For this revised edition, Dave Moore of Bristol, England, supplied the original text of "What Am I thinking About?" and John Sampas sent me the original MS of "cityCityCITY" with the different ending printed here.   D.A.

Initial publication data

On the Road

> Good Blonde. *Playboy*, January 1965.
> Introduction to *The Americans: Photographs by Robert Frank*. Grove Press, 1960.
> On the Road to Florida. *Evergreen Review*, January 1960.
> The Great Western Bus Ride. *Esquire*, March 1970.
> The Rumbling, Rambling Blues. *Playboy*, January 1958.

On the Beats

> Aftermath: The Philosophy of the Beat Generation. *Esquire*, March 1958.
> Lamb, No Lion. *Pageant*, February 1958.
> The Origins of the Beat Generation. *Playboy*, June 1959.

On Writing

> Essentials of Spontaneous Prose. *Black Mountain Review*, Autumn, 1957.
> Belief & Technique for Modern Prose. *Evergreen Review*, Spring 1959.

On Poets & Poetics

The Origins of Joy in Poetry. *Chicago Review*, Spring 1958.

Introduction to *Gasoline* by Gregory Corso. City Lights Books, 1958.

Introduction to *River of Red Wine* by Jack Micheline, 1958.

Statement on Poetics for *The New American Poetry*. Grove Press, 1960.

Are Writers Made or Born? *Writers Digest*, January 1962.

Written Address to the Italian Judge. *Evergeen Review*, October/November 1963. (Kerouac's open letter in defense of *The Subterraneans* before a scheduled trial in Italy, where his novel, published in Milan by Giangiacomo Feltrinelli, had been banned.)

Shakespeare and the Outsider. *Show*, February 1964.

On Céline. Published as "Letter from Jack Kerouac on Céline," *Paris Review*, Winter/Spring 1964.

Biographical Notes

For *The New American Poetry*. Grove Press, 1960.

For *New American Story*. Grove Press, 1965.

For *Attacks of Taste*. Gotham Book Mart, 1971. The question, "Which book or books were your favorites or influenced you most as a teenager and why?," was sent to various writers by the editors of a highschool newspaper.

Observations

"Among the Fantastic Wits . . ." Published as "He Went on the Road, as Jack Kerouac Says," *Life*, June 26, 1962.

Not Long Ago Joy Abounded at Christmas. New York *World Telegram and Sun*, December 5, 1967.

Home at Christmas. *Glamour*, December 1961.

The Beginning of Bop. *Escapade*, April 1959.

Nosferatu (Dracula). Jack Kerouac previewed F. W.
 Murnau's 1922 film of Bram Stoker's novel for the
 New Yorker Film Society Winter 1960-1961 Movie
 Series Notes.

On Sports

 Ronnie on the Mound. *Esquire*, May 1958.
 Three for the St. Petersburg *Independent*, June & July 1965.
 In the Ring. *The Atlantic*, March 1968.

Last Words

 Jack Kerouac's "The Last Word" columns published in
  Escapade, June 1959 - April 1960.
 The First Word. Kerouac's rewrite of his first column.
  Escapade, January 1967.
 "My Cat Tyke." Written November 1959 for "The Last
  Word" column.
 "What Am I Thinking About?" Published as "After me,
  the Deluge," *Chicago Tribune Magazine* September 28,
  1969.

cityCityCITY. Published as "The Electrocution," *Nugget*,
 August 1959; reprinted as "CITYCitycity" in *The
 Moderns*, edited by Leroi Jones. Corinth Books, 1963.